Steve Emecz *('Emm-etts')* was born in London in 1971 and began writing in the depths of the Australian desert where he spent three months travelling and returned to his native London where he lives with his wife Sharon.

When he's not writing he likes to travel and work on behalf of his favourite charity, Leonard Cheshire www.leonard-cheshire.org for whom he ran the New York Marathon in November 2001. A share of the proceeds of all Steve's books, in print and e-books go to the charity.

His cult leading character Max Jones crashed onto the scene in 1997 in *'Cut To The Chase'* and returns in *'Cuban Cut'*.

Steve completed the screenplay for *'Cut To The Chase'* in 2000 for Scottish Film production company Somerfilm who have taken the option on *'Cuban Cut'* as well, and are currently seeking approximately $5m in funding for the first film.

Cuban Cut

Steve Emecz

Paperback ISBN 1-904312-00-4

Published in the UK by MX Publishing

1 Clive Close, Potters Bar, Hertfordshire, EN6 2AD

For.............Charlie

Acknowledgements

The usual suspects can take part of the blame. The readers Daniel Morris, Paul Emecz, Carl Harris, Andy Holmes, Brendan Brien, Seamus Tobin, and my ever tolerant wife Sharon. Most of all thanks to those that called for Max's return.

1

The blackened-out Mercedes saloon sped under the bridge and for a moment you could see the reflection of the lights on the bridge in both the windows and on the dark waters of the Danube. The car was one of the more traditional 1970's style large-engined models with plenty of chrome to keep their drivers busy polishing. Across the river, three hundred feet up, the cross hairs of the night-vision sight of a rifle were fixed on a bend in the road. As the car slowed and came into view the gunman tracked the front window. He was leaning on the battlements of the castle which just forty years before had seen the beginning of a revolution. For a moment he lowered the gun and looked around to check that he was still alone. No traffic on the top of the hill at 3am. He raised the rifle back to his shoulder and once more the car was visible in the eerie green colour of the sight. The car came to stop fifty yards from a green car, which was parked next to the promenade. Two men got out slowly from the green car and waited. They stood respectfully with their arms crossed in front of them. They knew that whoever was in the Mercedes was worth the caution.

The Mercedes window on the side nearest the river rolled down giving the shooter a clear view into back seat. He checked himself as the occupant's face came to the window and beckoned to the larger of the two men. He had of course studied every contour of the face of the man he had been sent to kill but there was always that instant of hesitation as he mentally ticked the box. As the large man approached the Mercedes the man in the car reached down and grabbed a package, which he held out.

The package fell to the floor as the force of the bullet whipped the man's head back into the darkness and the approaching man hesitated, then reached inside his long coat for what appeared to be some sort of semi-automatic weapon.

"Karchi" he screamed across to his colleague who already had his shotgun resting across the roof of the car. They both looked around frantically to see what was going on. Although they hadn't heard the shot, when one of Budapest's most notorious criminals drops the best part of $1m onto the sidewalk, even the dimmest of criminals gets the feeling that something must be wrong.

The shooter knew he had a minute and no longer before he would have to disappear. He watched the next thirty seconds unfold with the inevitability of a stack of dominoes falling over. The next life to be erased was the larger man on his feet as the driver of the second car snapped open his door and sprayed dozens of bullets in the vague direction of the first. Two of the bullets caught the man in the chest and one in the stomach. The rest rattled off the car and shattered a street lamp, which cut of half of the nearby light. Karchi ducked, and re-emerged growling and emptied both barrels of the shotgun into the windscreen. The toughened glass cracked under the force but held and the driver's gun appeared with another volley of bullets. Karchi dived for cover but was too slow. The upper part of his jacket shredded as he flew through the air.

The engine of the second car roared into life but as it spun backwards it smashed into the cast iron railing of the promenade. Two more occupants from the first car stepped out over their fallen comrades and rushed toward the crashed car, machine guns blazing. The gunman in the passenger seat wielding a handgun caught one of them halfway there. The other got parallel to the driver's side and peppered the occupants.

Then silence. The last man standing lowered his gun and ran back to check on his colleagues who were sprawled across the road near the first car.

The gunman quickly checked the area around the cars and saw no other movement. As the first bullet slammed into his back, he staggered forward and grabbed the rim of the roof of the car. The last second of his life was spent with a confused and horrified look on his face trying to turn to see where it had come from, before the second shot caved the back of his head in.

2

The market had been deathly slow again for the third day running. Marcus Jones looked at the numbers slowly clicking over on his screen and forced himself to focus. He hadn't slept for two days which wasn't unusual for a broker, but pretty difficult to do without, well, a little extra help. Marcus had gone through most of the steps in the cycle. He joined the firm with the staunch belief that all drugs were out of bounds, then becoming slowly immune to the everyday stimulants like coffee and caffeine pills, then falling behind the performance of his peers who used any combination of speed, crack and heroin in varying quantities. He first tried heroin at one of the parties that cropped up every couple of weeks at one penthouse or converted loft or another. He'd worked through from 7am on the Thursday straight to close on Friday, and headed with a group to Battersea to a beautiful apartment overlooking the Thames. He had made a killing that afternoon on a currency deal and was buzzing.

Too much alcohol and lots of encouragement and goading from the rest and he found himself kneeling in front of the coffee table being shown how to cut a line. He had kicked the habit six months later after an incident with his boss. He often remembered back to how surreal the experience was. The fad at the time was for 'Pink Heroin' which was in fact normal Heroin mixed with crushed pink painkiller. The resulting mixture looked like sherbet, but gave a very different fizzing sensation.

Now he managed to stay off the class-A drugs but would admit to smoking dope to relax. He knew that there was no chance of him being as lucky again. The day that he had snapped two years ago was at the end of a 'Treble' – three days without a break – and he'd been called into his boss' office to explain a dubious call he had made on a short-term option. It began with a shouting match in the confines of his boss' office and finished with him breaking the poor man's nose. Marcus had played rugby for Northampton when he was younger and fitter, and his boss was half his size. The incident was brushed under the carpet and Marcus later found out that it was because the manager concerned had been dealing and didn't want to draw any unnecessary attention to him. He was duly moved to another team and made clear that he'd used up his only pardon.

At about 2pm Marcus's PC emitted a couple of small pings which automatically focussed his eyes on the top-left-hand corner of the screen. A small icon appeared with the NYT.Com logo quickly followed by a small cartoon-like character dressed in blue. It had the words "Roving Reporter" across its chest in large yellow letters. Marcus grinned and double clicked. A small video window appeared on the screen. The scene showed a large five level apartment block with a number of smashed windows and flames pouring out. The camera panned down to the street level as a group of figures emerged through the glass doors. A number of them wore instantly recognisable dark blue jackets with FBI across the back. Two of them were dragging out a figure by the shoulders and others pushing forward three more figures encased in handcuffs. Next to the video stream a text box appeared and as Marcus watched the pictures the commentary slowly filled the box....

"34th Street – the early evening light gives this wonderful City of LA a flattering haze but the relative calm of this up-market neighbourhood is shattered with the sound of gunfire. FBI agents, as we watch live, are just bringing out leading members of the Black Cobra gang at the end of months of planning. Our sources tell us that drugs with a street value of $50m were seized at a separate raid timed to perfection to coincide with this one at a warehouse downtown".

Pete paused for a moment as one of the FBI agents looked directly at the window of the shop across the street where he had set himself up behind the counter. Had he been seen? The man reached for his radio and Pete quickly continued.

"As ever, we are right on top of the action here and it looks like we have been made. I'm sure the pictures will continue for a bit longer as our intrepid cameraman has been encased in that mailbox for the last 48hrs! The man in the centre of your screen now with the wide-ranging tattoos is the head of the Black Cobras – Yeung Durang. He has been on the FBI's most wanted list for over a year now, and they have attributed (as yet unproven) over fifty homicides to him alone. It looks like he put up a heck of a fight judging by the state of his face. The man coming out behind him is Special Agent Johansen who had led the case for the two months since the previous No.1 agent was found executed in his home – thought by many to have a direct link back to the case. The Black Cobras allegedly have over two hundred major money-laundering schemes to cope with the volume of cash generated by their multi-level drugs operations. From PCP for bikers to high-grade crack for our bored middle classes, they had the city pretty sewn up. The question is that now the head of the beast has been chopped off, will we see the rest crumble or is there another charismatic leader waiting in the. .. … ."

"Hey, there was no need for that" Pete exclaimed as the miniature keyboard was yanked away from his phone by the agent half a second after crashing through the front door of the shop.

"Don't you learn?" shouted the tall angry man in sunglasses.

"Freedom to report" Pete smiled as at least this time they hadn't snatched the phone. He pressed the speed-dial for his editor as he was pushed out of his seat and against the wall. The staff of the shop looked on in amazement as the agent checked Pete over from head to toe.

"Yep, they got me" he laughed into the microphone attached to his collar.

"I guess they have sent a few of their lads off to FBI observation school. Though I assume they missed the advanced class 'cos we still got video".

The agent snarled and pushed back out through the door. Pete watched through the window as the agent grabbed a couple of his colleagues and pointed back to the shop. He continued as he packed up his things.

"How'd we get on?"

"Not too bad. You didn't quite overload the server like last month, but we got around ten million immediate hits. A couple of hundred thousand from across the pond too. Its amazing what a difference it makes when we get the break and it doesn't land in the middle of the night in the UK".

Oscar Randle was Pete's editor. If you rolled up every stereotype of an editor of a major US newspaper into one then you'd get Oscar. Early fifties, greying hair, slim build that came from chain-smoking and the constant nervous energy that keeps most editors bouncing off the walls. Pete had been with the paper for nearly two years but it was in the last nine months that he'd really begun to shine. It had been his idea too. A simple one at that.

Most people want to know about a story when it breaks. The closer to the action, the more captivated the audience. The internet had promised to make 24-hour news a reality, but you still had to update the web pages and you were still relying on the person being logged onto the site at the time. Pete's knack of being at the right place at the right time, which was more down to research than luck, had earned him the nickname of the 'Roving Reporter' – the boys from the copy department had made a bright blue T-shirt up with it on for the Xmas party. Pete had hit on the idea of linking the internet's ability to contact people with the transmitting capability of the new digital cameras and phones. The glue that was to bring it all together was 'Roving Reporter'. A piece a of software that people could download free from the NY Times website that put a link on the customers machine that would come alive only when a new story was breaking. That way you could be sitting at your desk at work or in front of the TV (if you had a digital set) and the little logo would appear. Clicking on the little cartoon character would get you into the action as it happened.

Despite a number of run-ins with the authorities, Roving Reporter had become a huge success. The "it could have put the investigation in jeopardy" complaint had come in a number of times from various agencies. At the moment the audience was largely New York and Chicago, but there was a growing following in the UK too. Pete had been a reporter with the Evening Standard in London before he made the move to the states and they had run a piece on the new media hot property in one of their Saturday editions.

"Are you heading straight back?" Oscar enquired.

"Not just yet. I'm working a lead on that drugs link into the Caribbean. I'm sure they're working through a number of the islands there".

"Take all the time you need. I'm looking for another break next week. Can you slip through three or four teasers we can use for the build up?".

"Sure."

That was the other genius part of the process. Pete's 'teasers' were lead-ins to the impending exclusive that would be sent out every couple of days until the story broke. It whet the appetite of the audience. They knew that once there had been a few teasers the exclusive was around the corner. Pete gave just enough not to give the game away, often withholding names and always locations.

Marcus grinned and reached for the phone. He was sure Max had seen the same story but he wanted to wind him up over the crap computer in his office he would have seen it on. His brother really should push for a decent bit of kit, but that was the Health Service for you, still stuck in the early 1990s.

"Jones". Max grunted as he picked the phone up. He guessed it wasn't a work-related call as it had been dead all afternoon and he had finally been able to crack on with the monthly reports.

"Hey little brother" Marcus grinned.
"What's happening at the forefront of medical science?"

"Oh its you" Max smiled. "nothing, much. Curing people and stuff. Which small defenceless country have you bankrupted today?"
Max didn't care too much for currency trading, and made no attempt to hide it, especially from Marcus.

"Touchy. Well it's a Friday I suppose. Did you catch your mate's latest exclusive in your slow moving juddering-picture format?"

"Yep. Must give him a call. He's due over for Easter in a couple of weeks. I must give him a call and check the flights. I can't believe he's been over there two years."

"And four years since you two were in Australia." Marcus chipped in.

"Four years". Max reflected. Pete had gone from local paper reporter to lead correspondent on the New York Times in the same time it had taken Max to become deputy-director at the hospital. Different levels of ambition he mused. He didn't let on to Marcus, or indeed anyone, but he'd followed Pete's career very closely. Read every article and watched every clip. You don't forget someone risking their life for you lightly, and they'd become close friends. Although they spoke on the phone and by email every week, he hadn't seen him since last July as he spent all his time on assignment. He was looking forward to Easter.

3

The moon was trying hard to squeeze past the clouds as the figure dressed in black from head to toe approached the fire escape. There was just enough light to see where he was going – the bulbs from the street lights all smashed or stolen. The rusty pieces of corrugated iron creaked in the breeze as he passed them leaning awkwardly against the bins. They were overflowing with weeks' worth of rubbish. A cat jumped across his path and he paused for a moment, as if deciding whether to go on. It was then that he heard the noises from the apartment on the second floor. It was the only one with lights on at two in the morning. The fire escape was also covered in rust and he took care as he climbed the stairs in case any were worn through.

Some commentators claim that Cuban policemen always dress like they are off-duty. The four men in the beaten up Ford at the side of the curb would back that up. Only one had less than three days of stubble, so you could safely assume that he was the most senior officer, which he was. Sergeant Fuentez grinned as a shiny four-wheel drive pulled up in front of the apartment block a hundred yards away and two figures jumped out. His hands moved slowly over the semi-automatic on his lap and he gave the slightest of nods to the other three. As the two figures disappeared into the block, the car doors opened in unison and they crossed the street swiftly and quietly.

Pete reached toward the windowsill above his head and feeling the cold glass on his fingertips placed the tiny microphone through into one of the small cracks. He turned the unit on and winced as a high pitched whine hit his right ear, and then the faint crackle of three, perhaps four voices from inside. Fiddling with the controls the voices became clearer and he thought he could make out the loudest.

Fuentez took the safety catch off slowly and motioned to his colleagues to do the same. The same scene played out around the world, would have the search warrant nestling in his jacket pocket but there was no need for such formalities here. The men behind the door in front of them were guaranteed to be carrying weapons and drugs and Fuentez just hoped his team would all walk away in one piece. His source placed six of Martinez's men and at least five kilos of heroin in the apartment. With any luck most of them would have been trying out the merchandise.

Pete froze to the spot as he heard the bang on the door. He couldn't make out what the shouting was about but there was a lot of crashing and banging making it difficult to hear. It only took a couple of seconds of gunfire to convince him that he shouldn't be there and he sprang up to run down the stairs.

Fuentez kicked the door in and sprayed the ceiling with bullets. The two men behind the table threw their guns out as did the three crouching behind the sofa. Five pairs of hands emerged.

"Marco you pig. Don't make me come in and get you"
he shouted from the doorway as he scanned the faces of the five but didn't see the one they really wanted. Two bags of heroin had split and the dust created a haze. Fuentez edged forward and the three other policemen stayed perched by the door. The tallest of the three scanned the room with the barrel of an abnormally large shotgun. Marco bolted from behind the table and raised his .38 in the vague direction of the front door. Before he could get a round off the shotgun roared and the blast lifted him clean off the floor and into the back door.

The full force of the door caught Pete in the shoulder and face and he thumped into and over the railing. Nobody in the apartment above heard him land in the rubbish bags though if they'd have stopped to think about it, they might have wondered what had got in the way of the door as Marco's body flung it open. The bags had broken his fall but he lay still apart from a small trickle of blood across his forehead.

The five criminals that hadn't been shot got to their feet with their hands firmly clasped behind their heads. Fuentez stepped over the debris to Marco's body and promptly gave it a kick. The low moan signalled that he was still in the land of the living.

"You wearing that vest again huh Marco?" he said as he turned the body over.

The vest had done its job though part of the shot had hit the upper shoulder, which was oozing blood quite nicely. Marco snarled through the pain and then promptly passed out. Fuentez shook his head and motioned to one of his men to give him a hand. As they dragged the body across the room he surveyed the spoils. His contact had been right about the amount of heroin, he could see at least six kilo-sized packets. These jokers would be back on the streets within days but the equipment seized would put one of Martinez's teams out of action for at least a month.

4

"Hey Martin!" Max smiled. He'd spoken to the old sage-like reporter many times when he'd called for Pete. It seemed like he never left the office, and always answered the phone.

"Er, Hi Max" Martin replied. He had really not been looking forward to taking this call. As soon as they'd had confirmation through that Pete was officially missing, Martin realised that there would be a few calls he'd not look forward to. He had already spoken to Pete's mother who had been very distraught.

"Is Pete in"

"Max, he's not here and there is something you'd better know. Pete's still not back from Cuba. There's been a few complications"

"Complications" Max didn't like the sound of this.

"Yeah. It's a bit difficult to talk now. Can I call back in five?"

"Sure"

"Are you in the office?

"Yeah. Talk you in a bit".

5

Martin grabbed one of the dozens of soundproofed 'interview' booths that were scattered across each floor in the Times' offices and closed the door. He keyed in the number for Max's office from his PDA and didn't have to wait more than two rings before Max was back on the line.

"What's going on Martin?"

"Well. It's like this. You know that Pete was on holiday in Cuba?"

"Yeah?"

"Well, it wasn't exactly just a holiday"

"You mean he was there on an assignment?"

"No. You know the Times couldn't be involved in any press activity in Cuba. Look at that team that was held there by the authorities for three months and they were there on an official trip to cover the Salsa world championships"

"So?"

"So Pete had an amazing lead on a story and was sort of unofficially following it"

"Unofficially? The sort of unofficial where if he got caught then the paper would denounce any kind of involvement?"

"Yeah, that kind of unofficial. And the worst of it he's there by himself as he's one of the only correspondents we have that's not on a US passport"

'Typical bloody editors' Max thought

"Ok, so what was he on to"
Martin glanced around the office. It was just after lunch and there was a lot of activity with people starting to get their leaders ready for the morning's edition.

"You don't want to know".

"Bullshit Martin. It's me you're talking to. You know as well as I do that if Pete's in trouble you're going to have to tell me the details sooner or later"

"Max. I'm not trying to be an asshole but Pete's really done it this time. It makes that thing he did at the senate committee look tame"

Max forced a smile. He had really been impressed with that one. Pete had got himself inside a cocktail party for the Senate Committee debate on party political fundraising. The issue had been gathering pace in the US media for some months and both the senate and the Whitehouse had been tight-lipped. Dressed as two waiters, he and his cameraman had followed a host of the leading politicians around the room as they joked about the stalemate they had engineered that day between the two sides. Both the Democrats and the Republicans had a vested interest in keeping the millions flooding in because no matter who won the races, all of them benefited from the exorbitant sums of money. Just imagine the effect on his or her standard of living if someone capped the amount of money that could be spent on a Senate or Presidential campaign. Pete had broken his golden rule and had run a two-minute delay on the beginning of the report for fear of it being shut down before any material got out. As it was, it was six minutes of fantastic footage before the security forces had burst in and pinned them both to the floor destroying tens of thousands of dollars of covert camera equipment. The authorities had initially tried a court injunction on the footage reaching the networks, but as Pete's transmission as usual had gone out live on the net there were thousands of copies flying around. CNN ran it as their lead on the six o'clock news the following evening and 60 minutes incorporated some of the sound bites, which called for an independent review to follow. Pete had been very close to criminal charges on that one, but as with most of the incidents with reporters in the last couple of years there were no votes to be gained in punishing the messenger once the cat was well and truly out of the bag.

"What could be worse that that?" Max asked trying to think what it could be.

"He's looking into a possible link between the arms and drugs trades in Eastern Europe and Cuba. He interviewed this guy on Death Row who got caught with a fishing boat full of crack off the Florida Keys. Turns out the guy's from the Czech Republic and got recruited to traffic the stuff out of Burma when he was there as part of a gang shifting arms into the country from the Balkans."

"So where the hell does Cuba come into it?" Max was frustrated and a bit confused.

"Apparently that's where some of their arms gang leaders went earlier this year"

"I don't suppose they were out there on holiday"

"I guess not. The links with Eastern Europe have always been strong and Pete thought there might be something in it. There was no point going to the Balkans and doing a piece on all the arms leaking out of there into Europe and Africa. That's old news. But a story out of Cuba, now that really would be worth having".

"No wonder he told me it was just a holiday. How many people know?"

"Just me and the Editor, but he'd deny it. The background story on this being off his own back is watertight. Nobody would find anything here to link it back. He's on his own on this one."
'And I know how that feels' Max thought.

6

The phone rang in the small villa and it took Easton half a minute to get across the sand and up the worn whitewashed steps. He picked up the handset and listened to the familiar series of beeps that signified that the line was secure.

"Easton" he said trying not to sound out of breath.

"Sir, I have a call for you under code 24"

'I suppose I've had three days of my vacation before they had to interrupt it.'

"Sir, are you there?"

"Sure. Code 24. Put them through"

"Hi Easton". Easton recognised the voice immediately.

"Max Jones" he replied.

"To what do I owe this honour?"

If there was one person Easton hadn't expected a call from it was Max. He'd been in the CIA for ten years now and had come closest to calling in his chips while on an assignment to hunt him down four years ago, when Max had been falsely convicted for murder. Bad things had a habit of seeking Max Jones out and Easton wondered what it could be this time.

Max explained as much as he could about Pete and Easton listened intently. As he did so he could picture the situation Max was in. A man with no shortage of history who owed a huge amount to the young reporter. Pete hadn't directly saved Max's life, in fact he'd done something more dramatic. Four years ago, when the whole world was after Max Jones, Pete had been the only one to believe his side of the story and Easton imagined that Max would stop at nothing to find his lost friend. Max finished talking and Easton began slowly.

"Look Max. I'm not promising anything but I'll make a few calls. We keep everything with the Cubans at arm's length as you can imagine. Most of our work is done through the Brits"

"Perfect" Max replied. "In case you don't remember I'm also a Brit"

"Oh yeah. Like I could forget. I'll do this for you Max but after that we're even."

"Thanks. You know I know you were only doing your job"

"Yeah. But it'll make me feel better" Easton laughed.

7

The buildings lining up behind the gate held Max's attention as his friend leapt out to sort out the day pass. Really they should only have one guest. It was unlikely that any guard was going to stop a Major from coming on the base for a game of squash with three of his mates. It was not like there was anything particularly secret housed within these magnificent old buildings. The naval base at Portsmouth on the very South East of the English coast was home to around five thousand men from the Royal Navy and usually a couple of companies from the Royal Marines. It was, however home to tens of thousands of transient seamen whose ships were docked at the port to replenish supplies or undergo repairs.

Three and four storeys high, the main buildings gave way to the small, more recent additions behind and the sports complex came into view. Jim's Audi purred into the parking space that was marked up for a senior member of staff. He was quite safe taking the space as it was the weekend and most of the top brass were spending the weekend away with their wives, or someone else's.

The man on duty in the leisure centre looked decidedly bored. Understandable really, as he was guarding a couple of squash courts and some showers. Oh, there were Coke and coffee machines in the lobby so technically there was something of value in the building. From the changing rooms Jim and the other two lads headed for court number one, but Max instead grabbed his bag and headed to back of the courts and looked for the storage cupboard that he had been instructed would be there. He took the key out of his pocket and after checking no one was around opened the door and stepped in. Some pretty dingy, though clean, shelving and such exciting implements as mops and brushes greeted him. At the back of the room was what looked like an electricity meter box. Max turned on the light, closed the door and turned the key. The meter box opened to reveal what did look like a very modern electricity meter. There was a keypad into which Max tapped the six numbers that he had been given and after a couple of short beeps the back wall came forward a couple of inches and slid to the side.

Behind the wall was what to the layman looked very similar to a lift. It was. Max stepped in and gave a wry smile as the wall slid back into place. The lights in the lift went out and a series of flickering green beams cascaded in a line above his head. The criss-cross beams slowly came down the walls all the way down to the ground and back up again. They would find nothing untoward in Max's garments although you could have hidden an anti-tank missile in his baggy jogging suit. His bag did contain an offensive weapon though. At least that was what Jim had referred to when Max had shown him his squash racket. Max's fitness level was a clue to the fact that he hadn't played squash for years – fifteen years in fact. Graphite rackets were the stuff of science fiction back then and Max's bag contained a vicious looking wooden contraption that he assured Jim had seen him through his college days.

The lift began to move and Max readied himself for the judder as it would no doubt plummet twenty floors down into the high-security underground office of MI5. He was to be disappointed as less than thirty seconds of ambling later and the lift had stopped and opened to reveal a very ordinary looking office. Baber was there to greet him at the door with that pensive look that Easton had told him he would be wearing.

"Baber, MI5" Baber offered his hand

"Jones, North London" Max grinned and shook the hand firmly.

Baber tried desperately not to wince. Easton had not been kidding when he described this man as big and strong. Needed to shift a few pounds no doubt (like about twenty) but he wouldn't want to mess with him. Easton had briefed him on how he had come across Max Jones and it didn't surprise him at all what he was contemplating doing.

'This is not going to be easy' Baber thought as he led to big man into one of the small back offices.

"I know this isn't going to be easy for you Mr.Baber" said Max almost as if he'd heard Baber's thoughts.

"Please, call me Jack"

"Ok, Jack. But I do learn pretty quick"

"I'm not going to pretend Max. Even if you were the most talented undergraduate at Oxford I still wouldn't be able to teach you enough in the next week to pass you off convincingly as the head of an Eastern European arms dealing syndicate. Lets just concentrate on giving you the basics which with a bit of luck, no scratch that, a shit-load of luck, may just keep you from getting your head blown off. We'll start with two days here then finish off in Budapest".

There was a solemn element to Baber's delivery of his little speech that had a sobering effect on Max. He had made his mind up to do this the day before and the reality he suspected hadn't really sunk in. Easton had called him in the car and explained that there was this Hungarian arms dealer who had been assassinated, but nobody yet knew that the deed had been done. When Max had asked how the CIA had known that, Easton had told him not to put two and two together as he was likely to get four. He had gone on to explain that the Americans has been trying to get into the 'Kovács' gang for years and that their chances were slim if head of the gang, János Kovács was gone. The delicate infrastructure of the arms trade would be shaken by the news. Especially so as 'The Nomad', as Kovács was affectionately known, was one of the world's most elusive criminals. Even most of his own men had never seen his face and the latest pictures of him were many years old. With him gone the rest of the industry would tighten their already close lines and years of work would have been wasted.

What had this got to do with Max finding Pete he'd asked? The interesting thing Easton had discovered was that Kovács bore an uncanny resemblance to Max. It was then that one of Easton's counterparts had come up with the beginnings of the plan.

He stood for a moment while Baber shuffled a few folders of papers and fiddled with a multimedia projector on the desk.

'Screw it. Time to become an arms dealer' he thought, took a deep breath and sat down.

8

Max stepped out of the warmth of the hotel lobby into the driving snow and looked across at the end of Margaret Island. He had an hour to get across town before heading back for his afternoon meeting on the island. He wondered why such an unusual place was chosen, but suspected Baber had watched way too many spy films and decided on a place with a lot of mystique. He headed for the No.19 tram that would take him into the very centre of Budapest. The bright yellow trams had survived throughout stringent communism, sweeping capitalism and the current delicate balance without a falter. Gone were the days where you could travel across the whole city for a single Forint though. Max paused as he reached the road across from the tram stop. His hesitation was spot-on as a large blue bus slid around the corner in front of him clipping the kerb as it passed. He grinned as it whizzed by. Budapest was one of the few places where concertina buses were common. Awkward looking single-deckers twice as long as a normal bus in two sections, joined by what looked like the middle section of an accordion. Hungarian bus drivers were famous for their speed and complete disregard for pedestrians. While zebra crossings were widely accepted as being merely an indication of a good place to cross, some felt these guys used them as effective targeting. As Max boarded the tram and found himself a seat he glanced back at the three men that had also got on. He wondered which of them was the trail that Baber had invariably put on him. He discounted one because he was obviously too young. The second looked like a badly dressed spy so he discounted him too. The third man was dressed in a long black cashmere coat with matching hat and was carrying a copy of Das Spiegel folded far too neatly in one hand. Leather gloves topped off the ensemble and Max suspected the neatly groomed moustache was either grown for the job or stuck on.

The tram trundled into life and slid onto Margaret Hid (Margaret Bridge) and made its way across the river. The Danube was a good half a mile across here and its icy waters appeared to be flowing fast. The tram stopped half way across and the well-groomed man got off. Too many others got on for Max to bother to guess and he looked out across the river back to the other side. The imposing shape of the Castle way up on the hill was difficult to locate through the snowy haze but his eyes finally fixed on the long sweeping perimeter wall. Baber's sources estimated (correctly) that it was that point just a month before that the sniper had chosen to take out 'The Nomad'. Max gave a small shudder as it dawned on him he was walking in a dead man's boots. The team in London had done a remarkable job with Max's transformation and as he caught his reflection in the window it took him a moment to register that he was staring at himself. Kovács' face was marked with two distinctive scars. According to Baber the one above his right eye had been attributed to a member of the Yakuza who had taken out six of Kovács' men and sliced his face before Kovács had discharged the tiny 3mm pistol he took to wearing inside his jacket sleeve into the assassins face. Kovács had apparently sent freeze-dried pieces of the assassin to the Japanese corporation whose ID the man had been carrying. After a month of that a truce covenant between the two was formed. Since then the Yakuza had brokered a number of deals between the Far East and Europe using their extensive Chinese operations. The other scar's origin wasn't confirmed but there were plenty of rumours. They ranged between the plausible and the outrageous. Max's favourite one, and in the guise of 'The Nomad' the one he would choose, was the one borne out of passion. Evanya one of the one time mistresses, a ballet dancer, had apparently opened up his cheek with a broken wine glass when she had found out about his other mistress. While she'd not been naïve enough to assume he wouldn't have other women, she'd objected to him going behind her back with her younger sister. Max ran his fingers over the scar and grinned. He couldn't claim anywhere near as salubrious a love life. One marriage with an amicable (ish) divorce the only major story.

The tram was now following the bank of the Danube and Max unconsciously folded his arms across his chest as they passed the houses of parliament. He could still feel the holster and shape of the gun against his side. Baber has assured him that the links with the Hungarian authorities were extremely good. Cynically he'd suggested that with the decision on EC membership still pending, they were being overly co-operative. Hungary had joined the PFP (Partnership for Peace) in 1998 and then NATO in 1999. Independent observers were hoping the current government would hold on until EC membership was secured, as it was much less likely if the resurgent Communist Party were to get back in. Western style capitalism had come with a price for all of the former satellite states and Hungary was no exception. With the new order had come Western money and Budapest had become the capital of organised crime for Eastern Europe. The fall of the iron curtain had begun the process of freeing up huge stores of weapons in each country. There will always be a demand for the tools of death. The movement of light arms mainly Russian built across to African states like Zaire, Rwanda and Somalia was well documented. Max had read that one particular conflict had seen Hutu rebels attack government troops with anti-tank missiles launched from their shoulders. Allegedly hundreds of Hutus had died as they couldn't read the instructions on the side and were unaware that standing behind the launcher wasn't a particularly good idea – especially when the launcher was being held the wrong way around. That was the tip of the iceberg as Max had found out. Many of the arms peddled to third world countries had not been tested, let alone maintained, with awful consequences.

A jolt of the tram dragged Max back to the present and he could see the imposing structure of the Keleti Palyudvar (Eastern railway station) up ahead. He would get off here and head on foot about three blocks to Beke street.

"He's got another tail" whispered the man Max had discounted as a badly dressed spy.
"What?" came the somewhat startled reply into his earpiece.
"Are you sure?"

"Yeah. Tubby guy in a green puffy jacket. Dark blue trousers and a woolly hat. He's about 6'2"

"Sure?"

"Yes. He's hanging back about half a block on the other side of the road."

"Okay. You keep on our man and Donaldson will be with you in two minutes to watch the other guy"

"Sir. We have a problem."

Marticell Denauvre had waited three years for this opportunity and wondered if he was just being a little paranoid.

"He's got a tail. Maybe one of his own men. Trenchcoat, hat, small backpack about half a block behind"

"No problem. We have another two agents in the coffee shop around the corner. Anything happens and they will be here in under thirty seconds"

His boss had an air of confidence but Deneuvre knew how slippery 'The Nomad' could be. This was the first public sighting in many years and they'd only got onto him through meticulous, some would say obsessive research. Getting copies of all guests' photos from all hotels with CCTV for the last ten months had finally paid off with the match that morning at the Romany. The match had come too late to get him at the hotel, and besides he'd undoubtedly have had a lot of protection.

Interpol had good relations with the Hungarian government that would be severely damaged if they were seen to have initiated a bloodbath.

Max walked up to the reception desk and smiled instinctively as he laid his folder on the counter. He had quickly found that his size combined with the facial scars tended to make people very uneasy unless he smiled. The receptionist returned the smile and pressed a couple of buttons.

9

Baber led Max into a small conference room and immediately Max felt four sets of eyes latch onto him. The room was laid out like a formal corporate interview. A small desk was in the middle of the room with a plain chair behind it. It faced two long large tables that had been placed together but at a slight angle to enable the four 'panellists' to sit in a line but still face each other. Max glanced at them in turn. No smiles. Three men and a woman. Baber introduced them in turn as they stood next to the small desk.

"The gentlemen on your far left is Dr. Axif Sanur. Dr. Sanur is one of the leading writers on Western terrorism and arms dealing. Next to him is Jeanine Jackson, a senior lecturer from MIT specialising in short quarter weaponry. Next is Jamie Callaghan a writer with 'Force' magazine and finally Paul Snow senior Eastern European operations for MI5. They have all been made aware of your situation and have taken the time to construct a guide for you, which gives you the rudiments of arms dealing. We thought it would be useful to get you in front of them for an afternoon at least. That way you should be able to digest the information they have prepared a little more easily".

Max smiled at each of them in turn and extended a hand toward the desk and chair. Baber smiled and headed out closing the door behind him. Max felt weird and a little intimidated. Not that he couldn't hold his own in a conversation but he could tell that the combined credentials of the people in front of him meant it would take all of his concentration to keep up. There was a pen and a pad in front of him but he opted to retrieve his palm and keyboard from his jacket pockets and took a moment to set them up.

Sanur and Snow on each end looked like they wanted to be elsewhere, Callaghan was smiling and Jackson looked like she was looking forward to the session.

Sanur cleared his throat in an 'Ok I'm the Chairman' kind of way
"Shall we begin?"
"Shoot" replied Max, which got a smile out of Jackson.
"We've been told that you need a crash course in arms dealing Mr.Jones. This is not the easiest thing to achieve. Arms dealing

has gone through somewhat of a renaissance in the last ten years and there are many facets to be aware of." Sanur's voice was tempered and deep and Max could see why Baber had referred to the man with a great deal of respect.

"The end of the Cold War left thousands of soldiers with little to do and much of the military equipment in the former Soviet Union and Eastern Bloc has, how shall I put it" he raised his pen and pointed it at Max, "fallen into disreputable hands".

"You're in the right place to get the ambience," Callaghan added. He had been a reporter for the US military magazine for five years and spent most of his time in the East.

"The black market in Hungary has never been stronger. It's sort of the gateway to the West for many of dealers and of course is the eastern capital for the mob"

"The mob is involved in arms dealing?" Max said surprised.

"Not directly" said Jackson. This was her favourite subject and she jumped in before Callaghan had a chance to add anything.

"There isn't much that the mob doesn't control. There is more money to be made in many less dangerous activities but inevitably they get involved around the edges".

"Like?" Max asked.

"Well if you take the land repatriation. Until a few years ago, the Hungarian government owned all of the agricultural land and ran them as huge State farms. The land of course had been taken from the citizens decades before. A few years back, following the exit of the Soviets and the subsequent democratic governments the decision was made to give the land back to the people. The records were no where near accurate enough, nor were the divisions there any more so they had to give all the people concerned 'auction' vouchers. They then preceded to auction off the land in small local auctions all around the country". She paused for a moment to take a sip of water.

"Miss Jackson" said Snow and Max immediately decided that he was either a stuck up toff or he had something quite wide wedged sideways in his mouth restricting his speech.

"Can we please stick to the subject?"

Jackson threw a stare at him.

"I was getting there." she snapped

"Anyway, the Mafia hijacked hundred of the auctions by approaching the people with the vouchers offering them various things to get them to hand them over. Many of the people were elderly so what would they need a block of agricultural land for? So, the Mafia ended up with huge blocks of land and in many areas engineered themselves a tidy little trading route through from the Eastern States. No matter what comes through they have built the infrastructure to get it through."

"So they guarantee the safe passage of those bringing the merchandise through?" Max asked.

"Yep" said Callaghan. "I've even seen them bring tanks over the border from Khazakstan. They have a huge network of farm buildings all over the country to hide them in. The authorities have their hands tied."

"Ok. I follow that. But how do they get the arms into Western Europe?" said Max.

"They don't tend to bother" replied Jackson.

"Their final destination is usually somewhere in Africa. No shortage of local squabbles and the occasional wider conflict" she added.

Max looked straight at Jackson and asked.

"So. Who are the players?"

"They don't play Mr.Jones" remarked Snow.

"Ok" Max sighed. "Who are the top five organisations I need to be aware of?"

"Just Eastern Europe or wider?" Sanur asked looking up from his notepad.

"Wider" Max replied.

"Well, my first vote goes to Black Doctrine" Jackson said. There were nods of agreement from the other three.

"The Black Doctrine are a huge group of ex Soviet Forces men and women who came under the leadership of a disgraced

General from the Soviet army in the late eighties. General Wartinichev is believed to have been involved with the Soviet Special Forces, or Speznatz. He took a division of them with him when they were mostly disbanded and used his family money to set himself up in Latvia and operates the group from there. There were no shortage of recruits from the downsizing of the Soviet army and they control most of the shipments from the Russian Federation."

"What type of arms?" Max asked

"Mostly conventional. A lot of tanks. He uses front businesses to launder his money and one of them is a haulage firm".

"Comes in useful lugging all those big chunks of metal around" Callaghan added.

"Sees himself more of a businessman than an arms dealer" Jackson added. "A born again Capitalist".

"Hard bastard though" Callaghan added.

"Oh he's that all right. Ex Speznatz, what do you expect? A community orientated tree-hugger?"

"Next?" asked Max.

They went on to three more groups involved in dealing around the world and covered them in much greater detail. By the time they had finished the third Max had drunk the two-litre bottle of sparkling water on the desk. They were all obviously passionate about their subject, as they had barely paused. Each time one of them latched onto the thread of one of the others.

"And the final group is the Kovács family" Jackson said and Max tried not to react. Baber had given him a detailed background on the family but it would be good to get this four's perspective as well. They covered much of the same ground as Baber had but Max decided to ask a few specific questions.

"Have any of these groups crossed, like for instance have the Kovács ever stepped on any of the others' territories?"

"They tend to stick to what they know," Sanur said and before Callaghan could interrupt "but of course there have been incidents".

"Like?"

"Probably the most notable back in 1988 Interpol busted one of Wartinichev's supply routes wide open and he had to get a lot of merchandise out of Poland very quickly but inadvertently led Interpol to one of the Kovács storage silos".

"Yeah" chipped in Callaghan "that 'incident' cost the Kovács at least five million in merchandise".

"Our sources put it nearer eight," said Snow and Callaghan nodded.

"What did the Kovács' do?"

Jackson stared straight at Max and he could see her pupils clearly against her light blue eyes.

"Kovács rounded up every one of Wartinichev's men and apart from one women, who he left to drive them back to Latvia in a truck, broke every one of their arms and legs".

"Ouch" Max said under his breath.

"Thirty seven men and women with multiple fractures. If the rumours are to be believed János Kovács and his brother did it all themselves with baseball bats as the others watched, knowing they were next".

"None of the other groups wanted to go too near the Kovács' after that" added Jackson.

"I'm not surprised" Max replied.

"Yeah that's certainly one family to stay away from" Callaghan added and Max felt a knot the size of a small orange in his stomach tighten. They decided on a quick comfort break and Max headed for the gents at the end of the hall. As soon as he got into one of the small cubicles he threw up violently for the second time that week.

10

As Max stepped out onto the main road the snow was swirling much thicker than when he went into the building. The trainer, a wiry MI5 agent called Heath had offered Max a coffee at the café around the corner and he'd jumped at the chance. One of Max's passions was good coffee. It was up there with good scotch and just as difficult to find. Hungary was one of those countries that didn't muck about. Ask for instant coffee and you get a blank look and pointed toward a small cup filled with a thick black liquid that will turn you into an insomniac in a couple of sips. Heath stepped out next to Max, tapped him on the shoulder and pointed him in the right direction. In the two minutes it took them to get around the corner and in through the café's front door they had both got covered in snow. Max brushed the flakes off his shoulders and walked to the counter.

"Ket Káve letzives" he smiled and pointed to a table in the middle by the window. Heath headed to the gents while Max sat down and grabbed the menu. The good sign was that it only carried Hungarian. Any place that included German or English would be used to dealing with tourists and Max didn't fancy that.

"He's gone in to the coffee shop with Heath and you're not going to like this, but that tail is on his way in as well"

"I know I thought it might be one of his men but I'm getting a really bad feeling about this. Where the hell is Donaldson?"

"Don't worry sir, he's already in the café"

"Well, get close. Jones has a vest on but that won't do him any good if someone pops him one in the head"

There were two goals that Dimitri had in life. The first was to follow in his father's footsteps and become one of the best agents in MOSSAD, the Israeli Secret Service. He was in a division called 'Metsada' – Special Operations. The second was to bury a nasty piece of crap that had caused his father's death. He was so close, about fifteen feet close in fact. He could feel the adrenaline pumping through his veins and rested his Glock 9mm on his thigh as he took a couple of deep breaths.

Donaldson was a very sensible MI5 agent but somewhat lacking in field experience. He'd been stationed in Budapest for the last three years and the most frightening situation he'd been in up until now was last month when the ambassador's wife had run out of Earl Grey tea.

Max took a quick survey of the small café. Before he got very far a very nervous looking man in a booth near the counter looked like he was trying to attract Max's attention. Instinctively Max reached down and pressed a couple of small buttons on his belt.

"Sir. Jones has acknowledged Donaldson."
"Pity he didn't agree to the microphone implant otherwise we could have warned him about the tail"
'Of course he didn't go for the wire' thought the older agent.
'Any cheap sweeping device would pick it up'
"Well I hope he's in safe hands"

As soon as the waitress screamed on seeing the larger Frenchman draw his weapon Max lunged to the left which was rather a good call. Two bullets from Dimitri shattered the huge window behind him and Dimitri cursed under his breath. He raised his gun and pointed it straight at Max as he staggered towards the space left by the window.

The smaller of the two Frenchmen had blocked the way and had his pistol raised at arm's length, the second's weapon was trained on Dimitri - the sole reason he didn't follow up on Max. There was a lull as the players took all of them in. Donaldson boldly stepped out from his Booth and trained his gun on the Frenchman that had his gun on Max.

'Shit. Four guns and none of them are mine' Max thought and raised his hands to shoulder level.

"Allez" shouted the small Frenchman and waved his gun at Dimitri who glared back and swore something under his breath but kept his gun on Max. Donaldson was sweating like a pig in heat despite the freezing wind that was now blowing into the café bringing the snow with it. Dimitri looked at the smaller of the two men by the door. He could probably take both but that left the one by the booth. He wanted this bastard but he wasn't worth dying for. He took another glance across at the second one and that was the chance Max was waiting for. He threw himself backward over the table by the window trying to slip out the gap onto the sidewalk.

The large Frenchman squeezed his trigger hard and the bullet slammed into Max chest. The force of the impact took Max through the open window and he slid across the packed ice into the centre of the road. A Lada taxi screeched and slid to avoid the body and slammed into the wall by the right of the café. Inside, it was chaos. Donaldson had headed for the door with Dimitri diving into a booth and exchanged gunfire with the small Frenchman.

Max grunted and gasped for breath. The vest had taken the full brunt of the bullet but it had taken all the wind out of him.

He got up to see Donaldson emerging onto the sidewalk holding his pistol in both hands. He was about thirty feet away but Max could see the terror on the man's face. Max drew his gun and planted three bullets into his chest and Donaldson dropped to the floor covering the fresh snow with splatters of blood. The two Frenchman prepared themselves to venture out onto the street. They were behind an overturned table and had Dimitri pinned inside the booth. From where they were they could see the sprawled shape of Donaldson's body and paused.

The Frenchmen's reluctance to join the man lying on his back in the snow bought Max a few seconds and was now two hundred yards down the street.

"INTERPOL" the smaller one shouted over at the booth.

"MOSSAD" came the reply and Dimitri threw his ID across the café from behind the booth. The larger Frenchman grabbed it. "Merde!" he screamed slamming the ID onto the floor. He grabbed his colleague by the shoulder and dragged him out onto the street. Dimitri scooped up his ID as he followed them out and ran straight across the road to a waiting white van.

Max was already out of breath as he rounded another corner. Up ahead was a taxi rank with a line of cars sitting with their engines running, their tailpipes spewing steam into the cold air. He ran to the first and opened the driver's door. The driver got out and was about to shout abuse when Max shoved the gun in his ribs. The man threw his hands up and retreated rapidly stuttering something in frightened Hungarian. Max didn't catch it but suspected it was something along the lines of 'Shit, take it, its only a Skoda'.

The two Frenchmen rounded the corner as Max pulled away and got half a dozen shots off. They took out a couple of taillights and the back window but Max managed to keep the car on the road with a little bit of help from a barrier. The wheels were spinning in the slush and Max wrestled with the steering. He rounded another corner and found himself running parallel with the Danube, not that he was in any position to admire the scenery. He eased up on the gas and looked into the mirror. A white van was careering down the road and catching up with him. He decided not to take any chances and floored the pedal. As he did so a car pulled out of a side street and Max swerved to avoid it but quickly ran out of road mounting the pavement. The pavement rapidly turned into a sea of people and Max swung the car onto a ramp to the left, which led down to a cruise barge. It wasn't wide enough for a car and the wheels dropped off the sides and it slid another forty feet on the underside of the car before it slammed into the pod at the bottom. The impact smashed the windscreen and left Max sprawled over the bonnet. He was a little dazed but the adrenaline gushing through his veins kept him conscious. With both sides of the car hanging over the water forward was the only open direction.

The white van screeched to a halt and Dimitri and three of his colleagues leapt out. Pistols at the ready they ran to the edge of the promenade. Max clambered over the bonnet of the car and crouched down just in time. Dimitri threw his arm over the wall and took aim and pumped half a dozen bullets in through the back window of the car. Some rattled off the bonnet and a couple thudded into a mooring post behind Max.

'This is not doing anything for my blood pressure' Max thought and pulled out his Walther. He ditched the nearly empty bullet clip and loaded a fresh one from his jacket. One of the Israeli agents sneaked round the wall as the others laid covering fire. As the bullets hailed down all around Max he took a deep breath. He swung the gun onto the bonnet and emptied the full clip in the general direction of the shore. The advancing agent yelped as one of the bullets slammed into his shin. He fell to the ground and began to crawl back to his colleagues.

Max looked at the motor launch tied to the side behind him. He loaded another clip and reached back to untie the rope holding the launch to the mooring. It was as the rope began to slip through his fingers that he realised that the current of the river was plenty to move the boat and it began sliding away from him. Another couple of bullets pinged around his ears and Max hesitated for a moment. If he didn't move soon then the launch would be out of his reach. He grinned and took a flying crouching start.

Dimitri glanced past the wall and saw Max diving for the boat. He got another shot in which slammed into the side of the boat as Max flung himself off the edge and into the bottom of the boat. Dimitri spun around the corner and began to run down the ramp dropping his empty pistol and reaching for the semi-automatic strapped to his left side. Max had found the ignition to the launch and it kicked in on the second attempt. He smashed the lever forward and the launch lurched forward. Dimitri took another couple of seconds to reach the wreck of the car and clambered onto the roof with his gun trained on the launch.

It was too far but that didn't stop him letting off a few dozen rounds that splashed into the water thirty feet or so behind the boat. He cursed under his breath that they had only brought close-quarter arms with them as the launch pulled further away. Max took a moment to look back and could make just out the figures against the shoreline. He could also hear the wail of police sirens and could see half a dozen police cars streaming over the bridge ahead of him. Dimitri had heard them too and instinctively sprinted back to the van. He slammed his fist against the side as he climbed in and the van pulled away with the back doors flapping. One of his colleagues threw a package out onto the roadway into the path of the oncoming police cars. A sports bag wrapped around what looked like a bomb. It was a bomb, but with a couple of wires loose it didn't pose a threat to anyone but it certainly looked like it and would hold them up long enough to get some distance between them.

Max scanned the other side of the river and could see a jetty in the distance. He had to get off the river and disappear as fast as possible. The weather was getting worse which although it was playing havoc with Max's sense of direction it was probably the key reason he made it to the jetty and away into the snow-covered back streets. He ducked down a side street and into a clothing store. Two minutes later he emerged in a brown, full length leather coat with a hat firmly over his head. The shop assistant had been surprised that the man in the expensive looking cashmere coat had wanted another coat and had decided to wear it there and then. Max dropped the bag with his old coat in it into a bin two blocks down the road and headed towards the underground station.

11

Petra had taken three hours to get home on 'that' day from the court. In the last eight days she had paid up her tenancy and moved across town to a new apartment and maintained a two hour trek into and back from the office. She was certain she hadn't been tailed and she had left no trace at her old apartment but nevertheless she was still terrified. She had thought she was tough as nails. Daughter of a beat cop. One of Washington's finest. She had grown up around guns and cops and the only thing that had stopped her becoming one was a promise she made her father on her fourteenth birthday. He had been wounded in a drive-by shooting and made her swear that she wouldn't follow him into the force. She could still picture him on the bed in the Maryfield hospital. Tubes and wires hung from both arms and he looked half the man she remembered in that familiar blue uniform. He had died two days later. 'Complications' they had said. So, she had kept the vow and in her mind did the next best thing and became a lawyer. Unlike the majority of her fellow graduates from Harvard she specialised in taking on the gun lobby and gained a reputation as a hard case.

It was Friday night and as she switched trains on the subway for the third time she wondered if she dare venture out in her new neighbourhood. As she pressed herself against the dim side of the carriage and sank her chin under the high collar of her jacket a couple jumped onto the train holding hands. They curled themselves around one of the poles in the centre of train and Petra saw the girl close her eyes, content in her lover's embrace. She stared for a moment then stood up straight and released her bunched up red hair from its bun and strode into the middle of the car. They weren't going to break her. She leaned out of the doors as the buzzer sounded.

"Screw you!" she shouted at the top of her voice out onto the empty platform. As the doors closed she caught her reflection in the glass and found herself grinning. Petra Harrison was back.

12

Max held his head under the cold tap for three minutes as his mind raced.

'Come on. Get it together!' he urged himself. He slowly turned off the tap and let the water drip off his hair before he walked across towards the hand drier. Half way there he stopped and looked at himself in the mirror. Not quite the cold killer he was supposed to be. Just some overweight guy with wet hair. He kicked the trash can which was nowhere near as solid as he had thought and it clattered across the white floor tiles and bounced off the far wall sending soggy hand-towels across the restroom in an impressive arc. Three of them stuck to the wall and this brought a strained smile to Max's lips. He shook his head hard and headed to the drier.

Within a couple of minutes he was back in the corridor heading down to the training room where he had a debrief session scheduled with agent Heath. As he was about to pass the conference room he had been in ten minutes before he heard voices from within. The four specialists were still in there and Max could just about make out what they were saying, as the door was slightly ajar. He stopped and listened to Jackson who was mid sentence.

"……….to the Middle East?"

"No. I reckon he's definitely up to something in the Eastern Bloc" disagreed Callaghan.

"Important enough for them to drag us all in here?" Jackson argued.

"What do you think Dr.Sanur? What do you think this Mr. Jones is going to do?"

"You mean you didn't notice the resemblance?" Sanur replied.

"No way!" Snow laughed.

"What?" asked Jackson.

"He's the splitting image of János Kovács" Snow laughed.

"Exactly!" said Sanur.

"But he's not been seen for years, no, more like decades" said Callaghan.

"You think that's maybe it?" Jackson asked.

"No chance" snapped Snow. "It's just a coincidence. I admit there is an uncanny likeness from the pictures of fifteen years ago but that's stretching the bounds of reality!"

Max breathed a sigh of relief. Baber had warned him to stay away from the subject and had hoped they wouldn't make the connection. These were good people who could be trusted but Baber had used the old cliché, 'loose lips cost lives' and reminded him that only a select few knew about the plan. He was about to walk on when Callaghan piped up.

"Hypothetically, say Mr. Jones was going to play the part of an international arms dealer what would you expect him to do?"

The question wasn't aimed at anyone in particular and there was an uneasy silence as they all chewed it over.

"Simple" Snow said solemnly.

"I'd expect him to die".

13

This was definitely a great place to see Margaret Island from. Max took another sip of hot coffee and leant against the railing. The tower in the middle of the islands had been there for centuries and despite being added to still retained some of its charm. Max had only just made it in time for the meeting with Baber and as he sat in the small lookout room at the top of the tower he reached into his jacket and took out the passport he was travelling under. 'Martin Johansson' was the name under the picture and Max smiled as he wondered whether he qualified as a schizophrenic yet with his three identities.

Baber was dressed in a Barbour jacket and from the moment he got to the top of the stairs Max could tell he wasn't in the best of moods. He checked the staircase before speaking despite the fact that he had closed the entrance door to the tower and locked it before he had come up. It may be the new millennium but $20 was plenty to encourage the attendant to go for an early lunch-break. He approached to about six feet from Max and stared at him.

Max smiled and drank some more of the hot coffee.

"Easton said you were a lucky bastard," Baber said finally.

"Complimentary as ever" Max replied.

"I wouldn't have needed to be so lucky" he continued "if your security had been up to scratch".

"Our security was fine. How the hell those boys from Interpol got on to you I don't know and we're still trying to identify that other group"

"I don't call six gunmen trying to waste me 'fine'" Max snorted.

"Where were your agents?"

"Well you know where Donaldson was" Baber snapped. "You were only supposed to shoot him in the chest once for realism. As it was you broke three of his ribs and the pain knocked him out cold. Why did you have to hit him three times?"

"Ah." Max felt a twinge of guilt.

"You put yourself in the same situation. You're an internationally renowned thug with very little respect for any form of life and you've just been ambushed. You really think Kovács would have left it at just one shot"

"Well,….mabye"

"Maybe my arse. I was a little concerned that the fact that I hadn't popped him in the head would look staged"

"Oh you don't have to worry about your cover, that's well intact. The wires have been jumping for the last three hours. Its not every day that a there is a running battle on the streets of a major European city that isn't gang related. Interpol are seriously embarrassed. The word is that they underestimated the manpower they would need".

"That other group wasn't mucking about though" Max added

"I know. Kovács wasn't, sorry isn't, a very popular chap" Baber smiled and took a seat next to Max.

"We have another two days of intensive training for you here Max and then we can get you off on the route to Cuba".

Max stood up and finished the coffee with a gulp.

"I don't think so. Every day I take now could be vital. I want to get on the way tonight"

"Mr. Jones" Baber got up and put his hand on Max's shoulder.

"You may think you are ready but you have only really scratched the surface"

"It's my call" Max said sternly.

"Well actually it's not. We have to consider your role in the overall operation".

"My role eh?" Max laughed.

"Just get me back to England tonight" he shouted over his shoulder as he headed down the stairs.

Baber watched the big man go down the stairs and shook his head. He reached into his pocket for his mobile and pressed a shortdial. It connected and a voice at the other end said.

"4-4"

"4-4. This is Echo five. There has been a change of plan. The package leaves tonight. Prepare the route."

He snapped the phone shut and shook his head again. The odds for Mr. Jones had just shortened again.

14

Max decided that the first thing he would do when he reached dry land would be to check if there were any links between the ferry company and a corrugated cardboard manufacturer. Why else would all the cabin walls have been made so thin that he could hear every moan and whinge of the family across the hall until three in the morning. He had never travelled on the Liverpool to Belfast ferry before, having flown the two previous times he had been across to Ireland. He had sensed trouble when the departure terminal turned out to be a slightly oversized port-a-cabin. It did have a coffee machine, which to his surprise worked, and only tasted as crap as normal machine coffee. Security came in the form of a young lady whose face piercing would have set off any self- respecting metal detector.

"Did you pack your own bags?" she had enquired
"Yep"
"Are you carrying any illegal substances, like drug or firearms?"

"No"

What an intense grilling. Once he had survived that, it was time to play with the car deck (floating multi-storey car park) – no simple drive on drive off concept here. Another designer with a sense of humour.

The cabin was pleasant enough, if you're into that sort of thing. Four beds (all made with an anorexic midget in mind) were laid out in bunk style with Max managing to squeeze into one of the bottom ones in the foetus position. After testing the bed he was pleasantly surprised to see power points for his laptop. He dumped his things down and headed for a wander around to check out the facilities.

Thirty seconds later, he arrived at the restaurant having seen all of the rest of the amenities on the way. That's a little harsh as they did have a TV lounge, bar and a shop with four different books in stock. This was the sort of ticket that had dinner thrown in and the menu was short but encompassing most tastes - provided you like chicken and egg. It was seven o'clock and they didn't sail for another two hours so he asked when dinner was due to be served.

"Possibly eight, maybe later. Depends on when we get enough people to serve it to"

came the confusing reply. Max must have looked as if he needed it clearer than that as the young man in a painfully burgundy waistcoat explained further.

"Once the food is out, it can't be put back – we have to have enough people to serve it to".

Fair enough, Max thought. With all the modern advancements man had come up with he would have thought more flexible food could have been available, but he was too tired to argue the point. He was obviously going soft. Just another hour and fifty eight minutes to go to departure. The first leg in a trip that would take him to the Caribbean, via Belfast, Frankfurt and Amsterdam.

15

Max had gone over the meeting a hundred times in his head at the hotel and dozens more on the way to the airport. Why they wanted to meet him there he couldn't fathom, but it was a public place which had to go some way to making it safer. This was all assuming he would survive the taxi ride. Cuba was one of those countries where all the old cars you don't see any more at home seem to end up. The Volkswagen they were in had to be thirty years old if it was a day, and the interior could no doubt tell a thousand stories. The interior trim was a 'wipe clean' mock leather in tasteful dark beige, and the door locks were those thin chrome ones that old cars all seem to have. There was no partition between the driver and the back, presumably because the driver didn't speak to him at all. The meter ticked away but Max had taken the tourist guide's advice and agreed the fare before getting in. It was hot. Max didn't usually have a problem sweating, but a man of his build in this heat with no air-conditioning is a simple equation. He looked once more at what he was wearing. Chinos, white shirt and a casual jacket. He had no idea what people in Cuba wore, so had taken his fashion tips from a coffee commercial a couple of days before. The ensemble was rounded off by a pair of boots and some very conspicuous sunglasses which he'd been given by Easton in a 'they-could-come-in-useful' James-Bondy kind of way. The sign for the airport showed two more miles.

Gorino was also confused. Why Martinez had sent him to meet the Hungarian he could not understand. Maybe it was deliberate. He knew about his late night partying and perhaps this was his way of winding him up. It meant he couldn't have a fix for at least another couple of hours, and he was getting annoyed. Gorino stood six foot tall but his slouching made him look a lot shorter. Despite wearing a silk suit, and an Armani shirt, he looked scruffy. He hadn't changed from the day before, and the creases looked like they had been there a week. Dark hair, steely dark eyes and heavy stubble he looked the part. Martinez knew he was an amateur though. Inherently lazy, with a cocaine habit he was only just controlling. His attitude problems made him a liability. But he was one of the cartel leaders' half-brothers. Sending him out to the airport to fetch someone meant he was at least out of the way for a while.

The main airport in Cuba sits uncomfortably two hours away from the capital Havana. You will find it fifteen minutes away from the tourist area in Varadero where the beach has a dozen all inclusive resorts, catering for anyone that doesn't have an American passport.

It is the type of airport that has one lounge, and in the country famous for its cigars, the concept of no-smoking areas has obviously never come up.

Gorino sniffed and pushed the few locks of greasy hair that had escaped from his ponytail off his face. He reached into his jacket pocket taking out a crumpled packet of Camel cigarettes and a silver embossed lighter. He casually tossed the cigarette and caught it in his mouth in the way he had seen in many films, and practised intensely. After the first drag he realised he had it the wrong way round and had lit the white filter. Despite the fact that no one in the airport lounge was remotely interested in his attempts at being tough and cool, he proceeded to smoke the cigarette the wrong way round. If you have ever tried to do this you will know it doesn't work very well and he finally gave up and threw it smouldering into the trash can next to him. It wasn't going to be his day. The half-smoked cigarette found a discarded newspaper and within seconds flames were starting to emerge. He ran across to the kiosk and bought a handful of cokes and put the flames out by pouring them one by one into the trash until it was sodden. Again, no one had batted an eyelid. Gorino looked around uncomfortably and leaned once more on the pillar.

Max paid the taxi driver and walked over towards the terminal building. By the looks of things there were some flights due to go out as the entrance had three tourist buses spewing out people and cases in all directions. A hoard of smartly dressed porters were 'helping' the bemused tourists get their bags onto trolleys for the long trek to the check in desks. As Max came through the doors into the departure area he realised that the aforementioned long trek was in fact only about a hundred metres. No sooner had the porters got to the growing queues (travelling time approximately twelve seconds) then they parked the trolley and looked expectantly at the 'customer'. Max suspected that they all knew exactly what "No I don't want any help with my bags" meant, but language-based ignorance was such an excellent tool.

Max looked around for his contact. You couldn't see for sunburnt tourists and matching luggage but the guy in the green suit stood out a mile. Most Cubans were dressed for the weather. Casual and simple but inherently smart and tidy. From across the terminal Max could see him puffing away on a 'smoke' and looking like a throw-back to the yuppie late – 1990s computer consultants who had too much money and not enough taste.

'Oh, shit. He's got a ponytail' Max thought. It was the only personal appearance decision that Max despised more than untidy beards.

"Excuse me, do you have change for a $20 dollar note?" Max said the pre-arranged line with as much enthusiasm as he could muster.

"Of course" Gorino replied grinning. He reached inside his jacket and pulled out his wallet that predictably was a flash burgundy leather job with a huge GUCCI tag. He pulled out 20 one-dollar bills, which was his agreed sign. Max thanked him and headed to the car park. Gorino followed a minute or so later into the sunshine, slipping his aviator shades on as he approached the white 1956 Chevy. Max was leaning on the car with his bag resting on the roof.

"Hey man. This car is a classic, don't be putting no dents in it" he laughed gesturing at Max's size. Max smiled and stood up and faced up to Gorino until he was a few inches from his face. He had maybe four inches in height on the Cuban, so he looked down slightly when he spoke.

"Listen. I chew up and spit out little shits like you on a regular basis. If you want to screw me around then I'll either waste you and charge your boss for the time wasted, or get on the next plane off this little island and onto the next place they have a need for what I specialise in. Which do you prefer?" Max growled.

To say Gorino was taken aback was an understatement. He was sure he had the hard gangster look down to a tee, and rather than back off he rallied.

"I don't think so". He stammered.

"My associate Carlos has your head in his rifle-sight as we speak. All I have to do is give him a sign and goodbye fat man". Gorino was surprised with his front, but immediately realised that this man in front of him would more than certainly see through his bluff and, despite all the practice, he couldn't draw his gun anywhere near fast enough. A tingle of fear ran down his spine as he waited for a reaction.

He wasn't the only one. Behind the mirrored sunglasses Max's eyes darted left and right. There was no way he was going to see, or avoid, the gunman. Damn. He shouldn't have been so bold. Okay, yeah, he was supposed to be this big-time arms dealer from Eastern Europe with an iron-fist reputation, but out here he was alone. He cursed Easton for firing him up to play the character so much.

Gorino's pulse began to race. The big man in front of him was surely going to do something to him. Would he really kill him at the back of a car park in the airport? Despite the very bright sunshine and the scores of people in the near distance, if he had come prepared with a silencer on a small pistol he could easily waste him without getting too much attention.

Max swallowed hard. Think. Think. Max threw his head back into a huge laugh. Gorino paused a moment, then forced himself into an uneasy laugh too.

'Damn that was close' Max sweated as he held out his hand to the Cuban.

'For God's sake Gorino, you wanna get yourself wasted' the Cuban thought as he grabbed Max's hand and shook it hard.

"Let's do it" Max said tapping Gorino on the shoulder and turning to take his bag off the roof. Gorino frowned and walked around to the passenger side of the car.

"Why don't you drive? I'm sure it's been a while since you've driven a vintage American car" he pointed towards the driver's side.

"Whatever" Max replied as nonchalantly as he could and climbed in tossing his bag onto the back seat. His focus for a moment turned to the dials in front of him. The position of the late afternoon sun meant the tops of the chrome dials glinted in a row in front of him. Whatever kind of bum this guy was, he sure knew how to look after his car. Max had heard that there were more vintage US cars in Cuba, per head of population, than anywhere else. The wonderful climate where even winter saw constant sunshine meant minimal erosion. Coupled with the fact that sanctions limited the numbers of new cars coming in and you had a formula for great old motors.

16

For the first hour of their journey toward Havana on the coastal route as the sun began to set barely a word passed between the two. Gorino was doing his steely, no expression on my face because I'm so tough routine and Max was trying to go over his background story in his head as many times as he possibly could. Gorino motioned Max to turn into the petrol station and while the attendant added the $20 to the tank Gorino disappeared to the toilet. The dust off the road had used up the window washer's tank. Max decided to fill it back up and found a half-full watering can. He lent into the car and pulled the lever that he thought opened the bonnet, but the boot flipped open. He tutted to himself and walked round to the back of the car. Max reached out for the boot lid and stopped dead. In the boot of the car was what looked suspiciously like a body bag. Max glanced over at the small shack next to the main building, Gorino was still in there. He looked under the bag and found rope, tape, acid and a variety of tools that he didn't want to even speculate about. Someone was going to get murdered, and probably tortured too. He shut the boot quickly, and turned to run but Gorino emerged from the shack and headed straight for the car.

He frowned at Max and pointed for him to get back in the car. They pulled away and after another ten minutes Gorino pointed at a turning off the coast road. They were not far outside Havana now and seemed to be heading for the nearby hills.

17

Petra Harrison wanted to punch the air with delight but managed to keep her composure.

"Thank you Your Honour" she said loudly and confidently and placed here file into her tan briefcase. It had taken three years and every hour of every day but at this moment it had all been worth it. She knew she had set a precedent as well. The Senate Arms Committee hearing a case raised by a small-town lawyer and siding with her research. The directors from the arms contractor looked dejected as they trailed out of the court and Petra forced herself not to feel sorry for them. Their prototype weapon would now never hit the production line. She was on such a high she realised she hadn't visited the bathroom all morning and due to her nerves had polished off a whole jug of water during the last mornings testimony. She hurried out into the corridor and into the restroom. She flew into a closet and before she sat down heard male voices come in. She glimpsed through the door and on seeing the urinals realised in her rush she had run into the men's. She quickly closed the lid and crouched on it holding her briefcase. She could clearly hear the two men laughing.

"Hook line and sinker"

"Yep, that'll keep the Senate off our backs"

"Inspirational idea feeding that hick lawyer with that report. Took a little longer than I'd have hoped for the little cow to get it nailed but she got there in the end"

'Hick lawyer' Petra thought. 'It couldn't be, could it?'

"The first shipment goes out on Thursday, four thousand units"

"Wouldn't want to be on the opposite side of those bad boys" he laughed again.

'Shit, that's Mark Duggan.' Petra thought. Duggan was the CEO of the arms contractor that she'd just got a production veto on and it sounded like they had already made them. Petra felt suddenly afraid and slumped onto her backside and began to sob.

'What the hell am I supposed to do now?' she thought.

18

Max had noticed Gorino getting twitchy and as they climbed higher into the hills and as Max had turned the lights of the car on he was getting more nervous. His passenger still had his sunglasses on in what Max thought was an act of defiance. Max kept his on too and concentrated hard as the sun disappeared and he could just make out the road markings as they wound round the tight corners.

Gorino was grinning and when they rounded the next left-hand bend Max looked down to see the handgun on his lap.

"And that would be for?" Max asked

"You were very stupid to come here by yourself Mr.Kovács. We know you have the main supply line into Eastern Europe but I'm sure we can deal with your people"
Gorino replied without looking at him.

"My people wouldn't give you the time of day." Max snarled

"Look. You can make this easy or difficult. You can tell me what I need to know now and bow out quickly. Or…."

"Or?"

"Do you really want to know? Most people regret asking that question."

'Oh, you do this all the time I bet' *Max* thought and began to panic. Beads of sweat were slipping over his eyebrows and he reached up to wipe them away. As he did so he knocked the side of his sunglasses which kicked out a small beep. Fortunately they were on a straight piece of road as the night-vision mode kicked in because Max's focus on the road was thrown off. From a dim outline of the road Max could now see every nuance of the road as if he were driving in daylight. He sneaked a glance over at Gorino who was still fiddling with the gun in his lap. Max's mind was racing and then it hit him. He could see but Gorino couldn't. He plucked up the courage and reached down.

19

Petra grabbed the half-full bottle of white wine and headed for her study. It was a mess with thick legal books strewn open covering the desk and most of the floor as well. There was a large noticeboard above the desk that was covered in newspaper clippings and yellow post-it-notes with her erratic scribble on them. She pushed a couple of the books onto the floor, poured herself a glass of wine and grabbed a note pad and pencil. Petra was a creature of habit and always planned her days the night before. She had to face it though; the last three years hadn't taken too much planning. She had spent the time divided between her study and the various courtrooms that it had taken to get her in front of the committee. She reached for the report that was marked 'internal' and headed up Axkon Confidential. How could she have been so stupid? It had been too easy to get hold of the report. She played the sequence of events back in her head. Bumping into the temp at that coffee shop around the corner from Axkon and finding out over a cup of coffee that he was working in the department down the hall from Duggan. Hindsight was a wonderful thing but she really should have realised that it was all too convenient. That he was drinking in the same coffee shop, that he tried to hit on her and convinced her to let him buy her a coffee. She shuddered as she remembered the weekend they had spent in that cabin in the mountains, where he finally agreed to snoop for her. Were they watching her every move? Was sleeping with her part of the assignment? She took another gulp of wine and sharpened her pencil in the electric sharpener on the side of the desk.

20

"What the hell?" Gorino screamed as Max turned off the lights as they flew toward another tight corner. Max said nothing as he turned the car at the last moment. Gorino's knuckles were white on the door and dashboard and as they hit another small straight he tried to reach over to the controls. Max grabbed the light switch and yanked it down snapping it right off. He threw the broken handle over at Gorino who had pulled his sunglasses of and was scrambling to point the gun at Max.

"Stop the car now" he shouted. Max smiled as he pumped the gas pedal as they went into another bend, turning the wheel at what seemed to Gorino to be the last second. He knew that on the other side of the very flimsy barrier was a drop of hundreds of   feet.

"Are yyyou mad?" he screamed.

"No. Well, I suppose yes." Max laughed.

"Don't worry, I can see the bends in the road from the road markings. Oh, I hope they haven't done any repairs recently" he smiled

"If you don't stop now I'll blow your head off!" Gorino shouted. He was holding the gun in both hands now and visibly shaking.

"You really haven't got a clue little man" Max growled. He could feel the fear and sensed that this was his chance to nail him.

"You waste me and there's no way you'll stop this car going over the edge". He continued as they spun around yet another corner a split second before the edge. For Max it looked like an easy drive in the midday sun, and he was getting used to the light orange tinge to everything. He was going pretty slowly at the corners but to his passenger the pitch black put the real speed right out of proportion. Max smiled to himself then noticed something flashing in the bottom right hand side of the display – Warning: Battery Low. 'Oh shit' he thought. He hadn't a clue how long that would last so he frantically looked across the hillside to see what was ahead. There was a corner with a lot of bushes coming up and then a long straight stretch of road.

"You wanna put that gun down," he said. It came out more of a suggestion than a question. Gorino didn't answer at first, it was almost as if he was considering his options.

"I will kill you, ..you pig" Gorino stammered. All menace had disappeared from his voice. Max wondered if it was his imagination but the display seemed to be flickering. As they approached the next corner he timed his turn so that the side of the car scraped heavily against the bushes.

"Oops. I guess the line was a little close to the edge there" he laughed.
Gorino grabbed the door handle with one hand the gun flailing around in the other.

"You are mad" he screamed as they pulled into the straight. Max saw his chance and slammed on the gas pedal and they lunged forward.

"Drop the gun asshole" he shouted across at Gorino – 400 yards to the corner.

"Nnno.." Gorino stammered as they flew towards the darkness.

"Last chance" Max screamed as he accelerated again. It was then that with a small click the night-vision disappeared. Max's world plunged into darkness and everything seemed to slow. He could hear Gorino blubbering in the darkness and wondered how many seconds he had before the edge of the road.

"Drop it now!" he screamed into the darkness. After what seemed an age he heard the clang of the gun as it hit floor and he slammed on the brakes.

Max was one of those people that passed their driving test and then immediately forgot all the statistics in the highway code. As they skidded toward the corner, rather than his life flashing before him, his brain was grappling with;
'You're doing fifty miles an hour, that's 150 feet per second, no, yards per minute, no…'
He held firm on the steering wheel as the car began to slide to the right. They were now a mere fifty feet from the edge. He made out the shape of the two trees a fraction of a second before they hit them. Silence. Max reached up and removed the sunglasses. It took his eyes a moment to adjust to the light. The

car was perched six feet from the edge of the drop with the passenger door wedged into a small tree. The back end of the car was about two feet closer to the edge, also nestling against a tree. All Max could hear was his breathing and his heart going ten to the dozen.

Gorino wasn't moving. Max wasn't sure if he'd fainted or knocked unconscious as there was blood trickling from a small gash in his forehead. He quickly reached across and picked up the gun from the floor. The safety catch was off. Max was almost relieved.

'Look's like he'd have done it' he thought as he stepped out of the car and saw just how close they were to the edge.

'Thank God for trees' he smiled and walked round to the back of the car.

'At least some of this lot will come in handy' he thought as he opened the boot.

21

Gorino had given Max the silent treatment for about ten minutes then saw no point in delaying the inevitable. He gave him the directions into the back of Havana, but stayed silent for the whole journey. Max had tied his hands and feet and sat him in the back of the car.

By the time they got to Marcelos street, Max's left shoulder was numb. He'd driven that last couple of miles mostly with his right hand and he began to lose all feeling in the arm. He guessed he'd trapped a nerve or something when they hit the trees. He couldn't claim that things weren't going to plan because, to be perfectly honest, he didn't have one. Max pulled up at the side of the street and he could hear the thumping beat of a Mambo band coming from across the road. Max motioned to Gorino and he nodded. The restaurant was smaller than Max had imagined. Max got out of the car with his arm dangling limp at his side and headed to the door.

You know that feeling when you've moved into a new area, you've settled in and decide that its time for your first pint 'down the local'? Except its not your local yet and the moment you show your face through that door for the first time it feels like the whole bar instinctively knew that the next person through would be an outsider. They must get an extra-sensory split second warning that ensures that they have the 'you ain't from around these parts' looks on their faces the moment you appear. Well, double that and you begin to get the feeling Max got the second he walked through the doors of the Club Juliet. Before we pause to consider this, it should be pointed out that a tied and beaten up member of the Langusto family had immediately preceded him through the aforementioned entrance.

Emile Langusto stared straight at Max across the card table and wondered if the day had arrived when he would regret the 'no firearms' rule he held so dear in the club. The man standing behind the crumpled figure of Gorino looked large and menacing and the long coat he wore could easily contain a formidable weapon.

"I believe this is yours" Max growled kicking Gorino's backside which sent him careering down a small set of steps leading down to the bar. The reaction was instant. Out of nowhere a medium build dark skinned man leapt the bar wielding a knife. Before Max could react the blade gleamed as it cut through the air and connected with Max's left shoulder. Max felt a searing pain – at least he would have if he could've felt anything at all on that side. Instead of flinching he grabbed the extremely surprised man who had followed the knife in and spun him around and into the side wall. The thud of skull on wood echoed across the room as the man slumped to the floor.

Max took two steps forward.

"Allesandro, you are really beginning to disappoint me" The comment was directed at a middle-aged man at the left of the table who stood up and held his hands open.

"János" he replied in a welcoming tone.

"Boys, back off" he added as the remainder of the Langusto family rallied and looked ready to pounce.

Max cast his eyes around the dining area. There were no customers to be seen. There was a group of four men in the corner some way from the main table but he suspected they were also connected to the family. Allesandro gestured for Max to come forward and as he did so he extended a hand. Max smiled and reached up to his left shoulder and grunted slightly as he removed the knife that was still firmly embedded. He smiled again and turned toward the door. Slowly and methodically he cleaned the blade of the knife on his trouser leg and took the blade end between his fingers. With a flick of his wrist the knife slipped through the air and hit the centre of the front door with a resounding "thunk". Max turned back again and took Allesandro's outstretched hand.

Max sipped another Mai Tai and the enormity of his current situation began to grab his attention. He tried to ignore it but he couldn't escape the fact that here he was in the den of one of Cuba's, and probably the Caribbean's most powerful families. Luco's voice broke the spell.

"Did you like what you saw on the DVD's?"
Luco was Allesandro Langusto's right hand man and younger brother. He was around six foot two inches tall with trademark dark skin and a very neat moustache below jet-black wavy hair. Allesandro was perhaps ten years his senior, around fifty and probably just how Luco would look in a decade or so.

"Some of it" Max replied.
In fact, he'd been impressed by the whole package as soon as his contact had been made with the Langusto family that

previous Tuesday. The disc had been dispatched via DHL. Max reached inside his jacket pocket and retrieved a sleek silver portable DVD player that contained the aforementioned disc and flipped it open on the table. Max was more computer literate than many men his age (just the wrong side of forty) but the multimedia set-up on the disk had him whistling through his teeth the moment he had first loaded it up.

The disc contained some of what Max decided was an obscenely wide range of military hardware available from the Langustos. The catalogue was heavily indexed and you could search by section or just type in what you were looking for. Max typed

TORNADO

on the tiny keypad attached and the screen came up with a full list of statistics;

Maximum Speed	800 knots
Length	17.2 metres
Engines	2 Turbo Union RB199 Mk103
	Reheated turbofans with integral thrust reverse

Beneath these the buttons PRICE, AVAILABILITY, VIDEO and of course ADD TO BASKET were emblazoned in red and yellow. The concept of adding a $10m plane into a shopping basket had amused and bemused Max the first time he had seen it.

Allesandro smiled as Max clicked on the video clip and a thirty second movie of a jet blowing seven bells of crap out of various inanimate objects filled the screen.

"Good choice" he smiled

"Yep. I first came across them when the Italians took them in 1982, and then in the early nineties with the Saudis," replied Max "but you seem a little light on stock"

"Light?" Allesandro frowned.

"I had my eye on half a dozen"

"Six?"

"Yes, perhaps settle for five and a Phantom if you're really struggling, though my client was pretty insistent on all six".

Luco leaned across to his brother and whispered something into his ear.

"I'm well aware of your credentials János, or should I call you Nomad?"

"Whatever. János is the name given by my parents. Nomad was given to me by my wonderful and faithful following in the press" Max laughed and they joined in.

"Well, János, you should appreciate that whilst your request is not a problem in terms of stock, the stock just has to be, how should I say, 'acquired'" he smiled.

A wave of relief swept over Max. In going through the inventory with Easton's friends at MI6 they had tried to find some items that would buy Max at least a week or two of time.

"And the amount of time required to 'acquire' the merchandise?"

Allesandro once more looked to Luco who reached for his laptop and punched away at the keys Max silently hoped he would have a fortnight at least. The various authorities had had a month to find Pete without uncovering the smallest of traces but he suspected they hadn't looked very hard. Journalists were not the most highly regarded breed, even those with a Pulitzer prize under their belt. He had to hold on to the hope that Pete was alive somewhere. His gut told him he was, but then his gut had had a dodgy chicken sandwich in the airport so might not be in a position to venture a strong opinion either way.

"Ten days" Luco announced with a surprisingly large flourish. Max tried not to look so pleased.

"That long?" he mused.

"I suppose I have other less exciting business to take care of in the meantime. I hear that Cuba has a few distractions to keep me busy" he smiled.

"And delivery?" asked Luco.

Max knew this was a critical question as six jets wasn't the easiest of cargoes to shift around.

"Well, I've got this small warehouse in East London" Max replied with a straight face. Luco looked very concerned until the old man across the table from him began to laugh. Max broke into a smile and the table ran into hearty laughter.

"Irony, irony" (pronounced EYER-RONY) said the old man and winked at Max.

"I understand that Qatar is particularly nice this time of year" he added.

Luco mimicked a grimace and returned to his keyboard.

"We must continue tomorrow, Mr.Nomad" Allesandro smiled.

"I see now why you broke your rules and came yourself"

"It isn't every week I get to spend $40m of someone else's money" Max smiled.

"Where are you staying?"

"Well, apart from the place down the quayside called 'concrete blocks around your ankles' that young Gorino had me booked into I thought maybe the Grande"

Allesandro looked a little offended and Max thought.

'Cheeky git. His asshole of a nephew decides to whack one of the most dangerous men on the planet and he gets pissed off at the man being a tad annoyed by it'

"Good choice, I trust you'll accept our suite with my compliments" he paused.

"Under the circumstances"

"That's most gracious of you" Max smiled as he got up out of his seat.

"Luco will drive you over" Allesandro motioned to the door and Max took that as a sure sign that this first audience with the Langusto family was over.

22

Havana was beautiful. At least the parts between the centre of town and the Grande on the seafront. Max had been to Cuba once before in the early eighties and despite some developments the centre has remained much as it had been back then. He wished he could say the same for most of his favourite European capitals. It hadn't occurred to him before but the exclusion of anything American had a whole lot to do with that. No fast food restaurants, no commercial shopping chains, though he must admit he thought he saw a branch of Bennettons flash past at one point. Walls and buildings were still adorned with pictures of Castro and Ché Guavara. Max didn't know much about the country's history but at that moment felt a twinge of admiration for the country that had resisted the allure of the west for a number of decades. They passed another Lada, the most common car on the streets of Cuba and pulled into the opulent entrance to the Havana Grande. The seafront area of Havana was mostly concrete and it struck Max as almost part of the luxury of the hotel to have the only green patch for someway located right in front of the hotel. He wondered if that meant the rooms facing the sea would have an even enhanced view.

As the doorman moved toward the car Luco stepped out and the man seemed to find a couple of extra gears. Perhaps surprised to by the fact that Luco was doing the driving. The man dressed head to foot in burgundy, gold braid and stripes bounded to the boot to get the cases.

The foyer of the Grande was a shrine to Italian marble and Max's steel capped DMs clicked as they crossed to the reception. As they drew nearer to the counter staff backed away and what Max assumed was the manager appeared dressed in a light blue shirt and very conservative tie topped off with a blazer. The man and Luco exchanged knowing glances. He handed the manager a white A4 envelope and introduced Max as their "distinguished guest Mr.Nomad".

'Almost extinguished' Max thought which made him chuckle and then shudder a little. A tiny (4'5") bell boy whose nameplate proclaimed to be a Juan grabbed Max's two large cases – one of the which Max observed was almost big enough for the little man to climb into – and they headed toward the lift. The lift was one of those terrible new pristine chrome edifices with built in 'patronising' voice. Not only did it inform the occupants that it was now 'on the ground floor, foyer' but counted out loud the floors as they headed to the penultimate. "Eleven, Twelve, Fourteen" Max smiled. The tradition of not having a thirteenth floor had been adapted for the lift as well.

A sound not unlike the "shhhhkk" of the door on the Starship Enterprise greeted them on the 21st floor and Max half expected Spock to emerge from around a corner, raise an eyebrow and quizzically ask "Captain?". Instead Max was shown to one of just eight suites that covered the whole floor of the hotel. It was rumoured that the top floor contained one huge suite that Castro himself was prone to entertain in. The lift certainly looked like you needed extra passkeys to get up there, and there were no stairs. Guests, of course, tended to arrive via the helipad on the roof. The lift was really just for the staff.

The door of the suite opened to reveal what looked like four rooms to Max. The lounge was probably large enough to have a half decent game of five-a-side football he guessed. He tipped Juan with US$ which the little chap made a point of grinning at, but Max decided that he was probably used to it from the guests. The Cuban dollar was more or less at parity with its US bug brother and most people didn't worry which they used. The buck was always favourite though.

Max set down his bags and glanced down at his watch. He worked out that the time delay with Washington was negligible and fired up his laptop. He sent a 'hey guys I'm online' ping to Easton and, despite the fact that it was the middle of the night in London sent one across to Baber. He changed into a bathrobe (heavy, monochromed 'Havana Grande' and definitely nickable) and fixed himself a scotch from the vast bar. He had just made it to the sumptuous sofa as he heard two beeps that told him that both the guys were online.

B – Hey chaps, London calling.

E – Washington here, what's cooking?

M – Havana, home to the anti-tank crew.

E – Hey Max, still mouthy even across the net.

M – That's me. As unpersonable in text as in the flesh.

B – What's happening, you've been offline for two days?

M – Unintentional, had a bit of a welcoming party.

E – Serious?

M – Nah – I'd better get to it. The Langusto's took the bait in the Hurricanes.

B – What, all six?

M – Yeah, seemed hesitant at first though.

B – I'm not f-ing surprised! We know he can get his hands on four out or Iran, but where the heck the others are coming from I'm stumped.

M – Well, the RAF had better watch its ass 'cos I'll have them in 10 days.

B – Ten!

M – Yeah, No Typo. 10 days. You were right about the clan – close family, but a few weak links.

E – We've had Luco Langusto under surveillance for six years now.

M – Seems like a nice enough fella.

B – Oh yeah, when he's not redecorating rooms in 'hint of brain'

M – He killed many then?

E – He's their hitman, and Allesandro's No.2. Our count is up to thirty where he's actually pulled the trigger himself. Careful as hell, he never leaves a trace.

M – Ouch – he's not a bad driver either.

B – Eh?

M – Drove me over here – I'm on floor 20 of the Grande.

E – Shit, they have bought into this one.

M – Yeah – took a little persuading.

Max typed as he stretched his left arm out which was now pounding. The knife wound had been sewn together by one of the Langusto henchman. That was one of the funniest things he'd ever seen. A huge muscle-bound frowning man in dark sunglasses reaching into his jacket pocket for a small needlework kit. He gave Max an admiring series of grunts as he didn't flinch once while the man set in a dozen deep stitches. The truth was that although he had been getting the feeling back into his arm it still felt more like he was being tickled than sewn up. Once sewn the whole area had been strapped – a little too tight for Max's liking.

E – I've left some more background in your dropbox – see what you can get on their missile capabilities

M – Sure, I know I'm here courtesy of your ticket guys, but I have a friend to find...

B – Yes, and we're working on that too. You might want to get to the golden sands restaurant tomorrow around six – we have a man in Havana – Tremiere – Anglo/French. He may have some news for you.

'Our man in Havana' Max thought. 'How bloody passé'. He could tell by the way that no new information was being handed over that:

a) they had some news but were holding it so he could concentrate on the arms.

b) they had jack and were keeping him upbeat by introducing him to the local man.

He suspected it was the latter as although Easton owed him he knew he couldn't count on Baber in the same way.

B – Max, you still there?

M – Yeah – I'll be there – how will I know Mr Tremiere?

B – Don't worry. He'll find you. You're not exactly inconspicuous.

Max agreed but Baber was still a cheeky git. 'That is always a problem for security personnel' Max thought. 'They always assume that everyone else sucks at the whole spy thing'

23

The room was dark apart from the outline of the three sides of the door which let a little of the hazy light of the corridor into the hallway. It wasn't enough to see by but the black-suited figure didn't need such luxuries. He'd been in a thousand hotel rooms just like this. Nevertheless, his heart missed a beat as he crept into the bedroom and saw the figure on the left side of the huge bed. He raised the muzzle of the 9mm Sig Hauer and pumped a couple of rounds into the midriff. The silencer did its job and the only sound was a small 'phutt phutt'. The sound of the impact was all wrong but before he could react a fist flew out of the walk in wardrobe to his left and connected with his temple. The Sig dropped from his hand and clattered onto the side table as a foot appeared whipping through the air and planting itself heavily into his chest. The impact took him back out of the bedroom and into a set of bookshelves. Clambering to his feet another fist came out of nowhere into his face and he felt his nose snap. His hands flew to his face, which was instinctive but a very bad move. A series of blows rained in on his stomach and chest relieving him of what wind he had left and a knee into his chin sent him out toward the balcony door. Sadly for him a foot followed at the end of a spinning roundhouse kick. Careering four floors the black-suited man drew one more breath before his body slammed into the trees behind the hotel.

It took Cassandra nearly half an hour to find a suitably safe location for the body and make the call to her backup team. Though she'd had to kill before in self-defence – it came with the job – she hated it, and wondered if the bulky man had a wife and children waiting for him at home. Moving the body had worn her out, as the guy must have been 220 pounds and well over 6ft tall. She was no slouch but its amazing how heavy people get when they're dead. She had gathered her things from her room and disappeared into the network of small streets that made up the Velado district of Havana. It would be too dangerous to return to her hire car – if they'd found her at the hotel then they would probably have the car covered. She'd been so careful too, obviously not careful enough.

24

For someone who didn't like firearms, Max was having some serious fun. The outskirts of Havana had given way to a wooded area that stretched as far as the eye could see. About five miles into the countryside and they had passed through a large set of gates set into a huge fence. Max was pummelling a series of targets with an Uzi that would have been at home in the mean streets of LA – or at least the parts that Max imagined were ravaged by gangs. As the hundreds of bullets sprayed the target he realised how inaccurate a lot of the gang films were. There was no way you could hold one of those babies in one hand at arm's length and get any sort of accuracy. He had both hands firmly on the gun as it peppered the targets but also the surrounding posts and structure. They moved onto shoulder-held anti-tank missiles with which Max took out a sizeable group of pine trees. He was accompanied by a couple of Langusto henchman and been shown a variety of small arms. All questions around larger kit were palmed off – they'd had their orders. Max noted that most of the people around were in military uniform of some sort. He wondered what bribes it took to get a military facility for the day.

Lunch consisted of some very tasty char-grilled chicken and lobster pieces with large bowls of steamed rice. Max tried to make small talk with the two henchmen but they made trappist monks seem gobby by comparison. He did get out of one of them that the afternoon's schedule was to be played out at the Langusto villa, which was, quote, "in the hills". Being in a foreign land worried Max. Being in a foreign land and away from the hustle and bustle worried him more. Being in a foreign land, away from the hustle and bustle, and shut away in the headquarters of the Cuban equivalent of the Cosa Nostra took him beyond worry. The countryside was pretty calming though. The route to 'Nirvana' – scriptural reference more likely than musical preference – took them via the coastal road before heading once more inland. They passed a gaggle of oil wells in two-tone green and rust that swung like pendulums back and forth. Max switched his mind back to the briefing with Baber on this, the largest of the Caribbean islands. The oil wells did produce oil, but until fairly recently most of the islands oil had come out of Soviet Union. With its break up the supply had switched to Venezuela. Max had asked Baber if he was winding him up when he had said that Cuba even imported milk, which came from Holland. Apart from the obvious cigars – high visibility, low GDP – the biggest export was sugar which seemed to make sense as all they'd passed since leaving the coast was miles and miles of sugar cane. Max had asked the henchmen their names and got No22 and No23 in return. He assumed someone in the Langusto organisation thought that it was terribly sophisticated, but Max thought it was lame so insisted on calling the taller one Bob and the shorter one Fred. He wasn't sure whether their resultant grins were out of amusement or annoyance, but at least it had provoked some sort of facial expression. Black suit, black shirts and black ties and the requisite Ray-Bans in this heat? A slightly retarded 'Men in (completely bloody) Black'.

Bob was driving, moderately well and carefully, while Fred sat in the other front seat turned at an angle facing Max in the back. The car was a black (naturally) 1958 Chevy. Max suspected Bob and Fred spent a good part of their day polishing the car, as all of the panels were shiny to mirror proportions. That didn't distract any from what these guys were primarily employed for and Max wondered how they were armed. As if reading his thoughts Fred reached in to his jacket holster and removed a rather impressive Glock. Max had learnt more about guns in the past couple of weeks than he'd come across from dozens of thrillers and movies. The Glock had a clip that held an ample ten with one in the chamber. Fred proceeded to check the gun over and fit and remove a sleek silencer that he had produced from his other inside jacket pocket. Perhaps he thought this show would intimidate Max but he'd gone past that stage. Max wasn't a particularly brave man but he owed his life to a friend who had now been missing more than five weeks and he was determined to find him, or die in the attempt. Baber hadn't understood that but Max just viewed it as evening out the odds. He'd had four extra years courtesy of Pete so in his mind he was already ahead. Max had never carried a weapon 'other than my rapier like wit – hah, hah' but today he had three. A shoulder holster housed a Walther PPK (and yes Baber had rolled his eyes when he asked for that – the same as James Bond for the uninitiated). His pen and lighter (both functional) clipped together to form a 2mm pop gun that Baber warned needed to be used at extremely close range. His belt contained cheese wire that Baber had insisted on, but Max doubted he would come across any vicious Edam or Cheddar on this visit - or perhaps he thought he couldn't bring himself to use it.

25

She'd seen the three of them leave the Grande that morning but decided it wasn't worth following. Two goons and a client that looked strangely familiar but no major family members. Instead Cassandra had attached a rather simple tracking device to the underside of the Chevy. She loved the concept of recruiting within the family. It generally created heavily committed yet technically inept pawns. She actually attached the two units connected with electronic tape while they had grabbed breakfast that morning. Following cars in places like Cuba, due to the lack of cars and severe lack of roads was pretty tough. On the busy streets of London or New York you can easily blend in with the traffic. In Cuba, anywhere outside Havana, half a dozen cars is considered a jam. The fact that the car had headed out of town, toward a known military zone was enough to change her mind. She had them on the tracking console now after lunch and they were heading out to the Langustos.

'This guy must be important' Cass thought as she kept the Lada ticking over at a steady 50. They were about 2 miles North of her heading into the hills.

According to Fred, the Langusto residence used to belong to a former foreign minister of Cuba, Heraldo Sanchez, and one of the most secure buildings on the island. Sanchez was monumentally paranoid and surrounded the huge sprawling villa with a deep moat to the South. Nature provided its own battlements to the North and East with sheet drops of around 400 metres to the valley below. To the West was the road approach across a ravine to a 3-metre wall with huge iron gates. At the gates was a security checkpoint, no doubt manned by some cousin or nephew carrying a suitably threatening semi-automatic. The gates had already begun to swing open as the car approached with the 'as yet unidentified cousin/nephew' waving the incoming Bob and Fred through.

Cass knew not to get too close to the villa and pulled into a side dirt track. She flipped open her palmtop and checked to see if Tripoli has processed the pictures of the European she had taken that morning in front of the Grande.

26

Luco met Max at the door of the villa and taken via a metal detector – the Walther was confiscated. Strangely, the fact that the other makeshift weapons had been left didn't give Max any comfort. The walk through the villa to the veranda was a gallery of dark-skinned suited guys doing their best Godfather impressions tipping Max small nods without the merest hint of a smile. The veranda itself had a generous sized pool with a bar at the end, which he noticed had the rest of the senior family members deep in conversation.

'Shit' Max thought.
'100% dark suits, and I look like a cross between the man from Del Monte and Dr. Livingston'
Cream suit, cream hat. 'The Nomad', he knew had had a penchant for pastel suits and while Max understood the need to stay in character he resented feeling like he looked like a twat.
"Ah, János".

Allesandro stood as he saw the three of them approach – looking like the start of a zebra crossing.

"Let me introduce you to the boys"

he added and began to point them out one by one.

"Andre" – dark, short and plump.

"Pauli" – dark, tall moustache, nice scar across the cheek.

"Tony" – dark, tall, ponytail, missing two fingers on his left hand.

"and Little Marco"

he laughed as they pointed to the huge man that was nearly as tall as Max before he stood up. Max wondered if Marco had ever thought of trying out for the NBA or NFL, or perhaps he had and they hadn't let him in on account of him being too big. Each man shook Max's hand though Marco nearly took Max's arm off at the shoulder. At around 6'8" and roughly at a guess 20 stone (none of which Max could identify as anything but muscle) he was what the phrase "built like a brick shit-house" was coined for.

27

Cass sat in the front seat of the battered old Lada staring at the screen with a stunned expression. The left hand portion of the screen had an unflattering photo of Max in combat greens with a breakdown of 'The Nomad's' illustrious history.

> János Kovács – aka 'The Nomad'
> Born Pécs, Hungary, 17th August 1955.
> First class honours Oxford, MBAs at Harvard and MIT.
> No.6 on CIA's all time most wanted list.
> Interpol file dates back to 1985 when he is rumoured to have brokered a deal for 40 T-80 tanks from somewhere in Eastern Europe (possibly Czech Republic) to the Yemen.
> 1987 linked to the terrorist groups in East Africa, mainly light arms.
> 1989 linked to the coup in Namibia.
> 1990 CIA file opened following strong association with parts for Pakistan nuclear program – a shipment of plutonium hijacked in Turkey.

1990 shot four times in assassination attempt –
gunmen and two associates (Indian) killed in the raid.

'Wow' Cass thought, 'The Indian Government sure didn't
appreciate his involvement in the nuclear race'

1993 briefly detained by authorities in Dubai but
released on a technicality (arrest warrant had a typing
error quoting a statute from 1981 when it should have
read 1971)
Net estimated worth $625m – mainly in haulage
industry, Budapest, Geneva and Chicago.
British and Hungarian passports.

'Now what the hell is he doing in Cuba with the Langusto
brothers' she thought as she clicked the palmtop closed. She
was well aware of Dimitri's hate of the man and that gave her
an added reason to bring him down.

28

What he was currently doing in Cuba was playing three-card brag, or at least trying to teach the rather drunken group of Cubans the intricacies of the game.

"Why do they call it 'Bastard Brag'" Tony laughed trying to look serious.
"Err, maybe the bloke that invented it had dubious parentage? "

They had begun playing spoof for healthy measures of rum and after an hour of that decided they could handle something a bit more sophisticated. All except Marco of course. The basic idea behind spoof (that of three coins each, placing 0 to 3 in your closed hand and then guessing the total number of coins being held. The person guessing correct dropping out then repeating with those left) was way beyond him. He lost six straight games before Luco suggested he dropped out. Even a man his size felt what was the best part of a bottle of Cabana. Tony had whispered to Max that Marco's nickname was Rex (as in Tyrannosaurus) – big, but brain the size of a pea.

'Trying to negotiate an arms deal when you're pissed is both inadvisable and difficult'

Max thought as he wiped his brow. They were sitting in a large long room with a table in the centre that at a push would seat 24. Max felt a little like an interviewee with him on one side of the deep oak table and the six brothers across the way on the other.

"So we are agreed"

Luco checked his computer printout slowly flipping the pages over as Max did the same with his copy.

"$2m to cover additional armoury for the Hurricanes and $5m across three categories of missile. Air to air, air to ground and heat-seekers"

Max confirmed.

"Topping up to the $50m mark with small arms as detailed on pages 5 through 11"

Luco added.

"Yep, that sounds about right" Max smiled. If it wasn't for the incident with Gorino Max felt they would have asked for a slice up front, but Allesandro had insisted that Max's agent transfer the money on receipt of the planes in Qatar.

"I've spoken to Klaus in Geneva and the transfer is cleared and ready to go" said Max and added.

"Thank God there's no VAT on this little transaction"

which was greeted with six bemused faces.

"Oh, sales tax" he laughed and the others joined in.

"I'm not too sure it would go down that well with certain of our politicians"

Tony smiled. Max thought he saw Luco throw him a stern stare and changed the subject.

"Well, János, will you be staying in Cuba until the deal is complete?"

"I thought I might make the most of the hospitality"

he grinned looking over at Gorino who was sulking in the corner.

"I have some clients to meet and my golf swing could probably do with some serious practice"

Max smiled.

"Well then, I recommend a course out at Varadero, not far past the airport.

"What's your handicap?"

"Apart from my habit of slicing, I play off an eight"

Max lied. He had played a few times but felt destined to be a habitual beginner. He guessed that golf was a given for an international arms dealer.

"Ah, with me playing off a ten that would be some match"

Luco grinned.

'Yeah, and you'd be over the moon when you'd do me by twenty shots'

They arranged a game for the following Thursday. Hopefully Max would be long gone by then. As they walked toward the front steps the others headed back to the veranda.

"Luco, I wonder if I could ask a small favour"

Max said and turned to face him on the top step.

"Name it"

Luco replied.

"I am trying to find someone, here in Cuba that I suspect would much rather stay lost if you follow my drift"

"Do you have any idea what region of the island they are in?"

Max had no idea, but Pete was last seen in Havana.

"Havana"

Max said in a confident tone.

"Ah well, that's easy" Luco replied and reached into his jacket pocket and retrieved a small stack of cards. He thumbed through them for a moment and passed him a shiny blue card with light yellow block print.

JULIUS MANTON – Chief of Police

Max raised his eyebrows and Luco laughed.

"Second Cousin. Just tell him Luco is calling in one of his cards"

29

"You are bloody kidding"

The young man said as he huddled close to the phone. It was raining hard and he didn't believe what he was being asked for. He hoped the rain was distorting and he'd not heard properly.

"But that was so much easier. They were being decommissioned"

The voice on the other end of the line became sharp.

"We can always find ourselves another source" he snapped.

"Okay, okay but I'll need a month. I'm not a magician"

"You have a week" the man snapped and put the phone down. He began to protest but realised there was no one at the other end. He slammed the phone down and gave the base a kick. He looked three blocks down to the grey building and began to make his way back shaking his head from side to side.

30

They were on the move again. Cass waited two minutes after the sleek back car had passed her on the road and pulled the Lada out sending wisps of dust up into the air. It was four-thirty. He'd been at the villa for three hours. They were heading back into Havana and she decided to take the inland route back to the Grande hotel.

"Oh and book me a room at the Grande" she added "as high up as possible".

She held on the line while her colleague made the booking.

"Floor 18 – the best I could do"

Tamian was very efficient and a good agent but persistently making advances.

"I don't suppose you want some company"

Cass cringed but decided to be polite.

"Much as I would enjoy your charm Tam, I need to stay focussed, especially after last night".

"I suppose so. The colonel is very concerned about you getting made"

"Ah, that's very sweet but he need not worry. I've picked up a fresh passport and cut and dyed my hair"

"Oh, not your hair surely!"

"Yup. Had to go one day" Cass laughed running her hand through the jet-black hair that now barely touched her shoulders. Since she had been a child she had long flowing hair to her waist and she felt somehow naked without it. It was a straight piece of road and Cass stole a peek at herself in the mirror.

'I suppose it'll dry faster' she smiled to herself.

31

Max walked through the front doors of the police station and couldn't help wondering if this is how a cat would feel wandering the corridors of Battersea Dog Home. Cuban policemen seemed very laid back and he wondered whether Havana suffered much from crime. In fact, apart from a few established syndicates Cuba was relatively crime free. The large man behind the counter asked Max what he wanted in the time-honoured tradition of all desk sergeants. He looked up from his pad and raised an eyebrow about half an inch with a 'Yeah?' look on his face.

"Julius Manton"

Max said pronouncing it just the way Luis had. The man's expression changed ever so slightly to 'Oh, ok?' and picked up the phone.

"Captain.................." he said in a monotone. Max's Cuban was poor but he was sure the man said the word 'ice' in there somewhere.

"A man dressed like an ice cream?" Julius Manton laughed the kind of barrel laugh you'd associate with, well, a barrel shaped man. He was a little on the plump side from the last fifteen years driving a desk, but nevertheless the laugh didn't quite fit him.

"Send him in" he laughed again.

The sergeant nodded and pointed to a corridor off to the left then held up three fingers. Max set off down the corridor before he got to the third door a tall broad shouldered man with a dark blue uniform stepped out into the corridor.

"Not many people ask for me by name"

he smiled holding out his hand. Max removed his hat, shook his hand and replied.

"Kovács. János Kovács."

"Mr Kovács, please come in"

Manton showed Max into his office that was fairly roomy with two small leather settees facing a large carved desk. The walls were covered in paintings and photographs, mostly black and white of Castro and what Max assumed were high-ranking politicians.

"Iced Tea?"

Manton asked and gestured for Max to sit in the nearer settee. Max wiped the sweat off his brow.

"Thankyou"

he smiled a little relieved. He hadn't got used to the heat. Manton reached into his sideboard behind the desk that contained a small fridge. From it he produced a jug of iced lemon tea and a couple of frosted glasses.

"So what can I do for you, Mr Kovács?"

"I was referred to you by Luco Langusto"

At the name Manton's face became a little more serious.

"He said you owed him a favour" Max paused

"or two, and I happen to be in need of a favour" he smiled.

"He did, did he?" Manton eyed Max up and down warily.

"Well, although I'm familiar with Senor Langusto, my dealings with him have been extremely limited" Max felt his hopes slide.

"However, as a welcome guest of our country" Manton winked "I am happy to oblige you within the scope of my normal duties".

Max breathed deeply in and out. He reached into his pocket and retrieved a 6"x4" card with Pete's picture and vital statistics. He'd run off a couple of hundred through a mate of his at print studio.

"Pete Smalt" Manton read off the card. "And you believe he is in Cuba?"

"He was last seen in Havana about five weeks ago"

Manton slowly shook his head.

"Mr.Kovács. I assume someone has already explained that for missing persons the first 48hrs are critical. After one or two weeks the chances of finding someone are small at best. I see that the young man in question is a journalist"

"Yeah. New York Times, though he's English I think"

"He was here on holiday or working a story"

"He was working a story and the reason I need to find him is that he may have some 'research' "– Max motioned quote marks with his fingers – "that could be somewhat damaging to my organisation"

"I see. What is it that you do Mr.Kovács?"

"Import-Export" Max smiled.

"Ah" smiled Manton seeing the connection with his cousin. Although he didn't agree with what Luco and the other family members were involved in, he couldn't judge as his growing pension fund wasn't completely from the right side of the fence.

"Anyone else looked for him?"

"Yes, sort of. You might want to check with the British Embassy for records. I'm sure they have them but I'm not in a position to gain access"

"OK, I make no promises but we'll do our best. What value would you say such information would be to your organisation?"

'Oh here it comes' Max thought. He lent forward and scribbled $5,000 onto the deskpad. Manton sighed and added a 1 to the front, $15,000, and looked at Max with a questioning look. Max felt nautious at the fact that he was bidding for information to find his friend. The fact was that Max's budget was limited. His basic expenses were being covered by MI6 and the CIA in return for the information on the Langustos and bribe money had to come from his own coffers. He'd sold some investments and a quick re-mortgage had freed up a chunk but at $15k a time that wouldn't last long. Max paused, leaned over and changed the 5 to a 0, hoping he wouldn't piss off Manton. $10,000 Manton wrote and smiled.

"And your mobile number?"

Max wrote it on the pad.

"Thank you" he said. As he headed towards the door with a sheet from the pad which had a set of numbers to a Swiss bank account.

32

Max headed back to the Grande in a taxi and was in a bit of a subdued mood. He hadn't made that much progress and the meeting with Manton hadn't exactly filled him with confidence. As he headed up in the lift he wondered if he had bitten off more than he could chew. He stepped out onto the 20th floor and immediately realised something was wrong but couldn't put his finger on it.

Cass had made it to the Grande ten minutes before Max and after a quick change of outfit in her room went up the four flights of stairs to the twentieth in her cleaners outfit. She found a cart at the end of the corridor and made her way towards the lift.

As Max stepped out of the lift the first thing he saw was the cleaner and her cart. He smiled and walked towards her as his room was at the end of the corridor – he still couldn't figure out what was wrong. Cass smiled back and had her hand on her pistol underneath the pile of towels in front of her.

Max looked past the cleaner as a large man dressed in black turned the corner dressed in a long black coat. Cass felt the barrel of the shotgun in the small of her back and froze. Max paused and looked at the scene in front of him.

"Back off Senor. This doesn't concern you," said the man slowly.

"Botchanot, en nem besselek Angolul" 'Sorry I don't speak English' Max said and carried on walking. Two more steps and he could see the gun.

The man in black swung the butt of the shotgun against the back of Cass' head and she flopped onto the cart.

"I said back off" shouted the man at Max and pointed the shotgun at his stomach from ten feet away.

Max stopped and waited. He had guessed it might come to this. If he was going to die then at least he would go out fighting. He smiled and the man looked confused. He threw himself forward and landed on the front of the cart that shot backward into the man's stomach. The shotgun clattered on the floor and Max dove for it. The man in black scrambled backwards and around the corner. Max headed after him and fired towards the fire exit as the man pushed through the door. He heard a scream and a thump. He reached the stairwell and pushed the door. The shotgun had taken a chunk out of the frame and judging by the crumpled heap at the bottom of the stairs, out of him too.

"Damn!" Max said loudly then realised that there was an innocent unconscious cleaner in the hallway and ran back. The woman was lying on her back and as Max bent down he saw the pistol in her hand.

"Damn!" he said again.

33

Cass's head was pounding. She opened her eyes slowly. She was propped up sitting on her bed, at least she thought it was her bed, it looked like her bed.

"Hey" Max said and threw her some ice wrapped in flannel.

"Hey?" she replied slowly.

"Coffee's by the side of the bed. You want to explain what you were doing with a gun and dressed as a cleaner?"

"Oh". Cass didn't know what to say. Things like this didn't happen in her profession. Cold blooded arms dealers didn't make you coffee and ask you questions.

Max was sitting at the small table and waved his pistol.

"Well, I'm here to arrest a pig of an arms dealer call Kovács, and I guess that must be you" she snapped.

"Arrest?" Max said, "You're from the Cuban police?"

"No" Cass smiled. "Mossad".

'Oh shit' Max thought.

"So get it over with you bastard because you are not going to have your way with me" she growled.

"Ah." Max replied. There was no way he was going to get out of this easily.

"Here's the thing. Let's just say for argument that I wasn't exactly the man you think I am"

"Oh, yeah sure, János Kovács is a real nice guy" Cass laughed.

"János Kovács is dead," Max said flatly.

"You look pretty alive to me" Cass replied.

"How much do you know about János Kovács?"

"Enough to know you fit the bill" Cass snapped.

"Do you know what he has on his left shoulder blade?"

"Er, a tattoo of a black panther"

Max stood up and removed his shirt.

"That doesn't prove anything. Tattoos can be removed" Cass argued but Max could tell there was doubt in her voice.

"Okay, would János Kovács do this?" he smiled and threw his pistol over onto the bed next to Cass. She grabbed it and checked the magazine. The clip was full. She pointed the gun back at Max.

"So. You have my attention. Make the story a good one."

Max talked for half an hour straight. He started with the background on how he met Pete back in Oxfordshire while he had been on the run. Max had been framed for murder four years before and despite only meeting him by chance, Pete had stuck by Max across two continents and through a bunch of dangerous situations. Pete and Max had travelled across Australia to get the evidence needed to clear Max and had even had some dealings with the CIA. Cass interrupted Max a couple of times to get him to repeat certain parts of the story. If he didn't come across so genuine she wouldn't have believed him. When he finally finished he looked at her and smiled.

"What now?" he said.

"I could really do with something to eat?" She replied.

"Sure" Max said relieved.

"I'll tell you what. You freshen up while I go and sort out your friend from earlier"

"You've got the guy from the corridor. That's great. I really want to get some information from him." Cass replied jumping up from the bed and heading towards the door.

Max put his arm out to stop her.

"Sorry. The only thing I'm going to get from him is a hernia. He's a heavy bastard. It's funny, is it me or do dead guys weigh more"

"Shit. I could really do with finding out how Martinez is keeping tabs on me," Cass said.

"Next time I'll aim for the legs, ok?" Max said over his shoulder as he walked out of the door.

34

Max was more nervous about the fact that he hadn't had a decent nights sleep in the last two weeks than the fact that he was in a busy restaurant. The Uno Habana was a magnificent building that had been used in many ways over the three centuries since it had been built. Its most decadent feature being the huge glass domes, six in all that gave it such an amazing level of light. This last iteration as a restaurant followed a particularly successful reign as Havana's main musical venue. Evidence of that remained with wonderful prints of Salsa dancers and grinning musicians which adorned the walls. Max smiled. His ex-wife had insisted he joined in the Salsa craze that had swept North London in the late 90s. He had managed to get quite good. Not from natural ability but from a pig-headed stubbornness that saw him get through a host of dance partners. His wife had had enough after the second broken toe and refused to dance with him until he had mastered the difficult moves. Such a shame really, they had only squeezed in three or four evenings on the hardwood before the divorce came along. Were they still friends? Hardly, they had even less in common now then when they were married, which didn't stretch too much beyond sharing a name - and with a name like Jones it wasn't exactly exotic enough to want to hold on to either. There was no animosity created by large alimony payments. Mary was an accomplished lawyer and had always earned more than him and there were no kids to complicate matters.

He looked at Cass and smiled. She was studying the menu and he couldn't help focusing on those lips. She was wearing a print dress that was very well cut for her slender figure but flowing enough to conceal the undoubted arsenal she had strapped to herself at the hotel. The walls in the small motel were thin enough for Max to have been able to hear her getting ready in the morning and was in no doubt that she had more than the single pistol that he had inside his jacket.

The waiter ambled up to the table and Max realised that having spent the past few minutes staring at Cass he had no idea what was on the menu. He didn't really need to look, as variety was not a word Max would associate with Cuban cuisine.

"Mademoiselle?" the waiter enquired. French was not the mainstay here and it irritated Max that the guy was trying to be hip. He looked a little funny too. Max couldn't quite put his finger on it but he was sure there was something amiss.

"Chicken Salad please" Cass smiled

"I'll go for the same" Max added and looked straight into the waiter's eyes. This drew no reaction apart from a cursory "Oui Monsieur" and the waiter headed for the kitchen.

"There's something about that waiter" they both said under their breath and then laughed.

"Apart from the bad accent and the hairstyle that is definitely looks like a Syrup, there's something else"

"Syrup?" Cass smiled.

"Oh, hair-piece, Syrup and Fig......wig. Rhyming slang" Max replied. He must try to avoid colloquialisms like that. Cass's English was excellent but she'd be hard pressed to have picked up that one.

"You think?"

"Possibly, though he had better have kept the receipt because one day he'll look in a mirror and realise he looks like a 1980s footballer"

"Ah yes, Glenn Hoddle" Cass winked and it was Max's turn to be surprised.

"Don't' tell me you're a Spurs fan?" he asked in mock horror.

"No. My brother studied in London and would always take me to games when I visited him"

"Makes sense, but why Spurs?"

"Oh no, not just Tottenham. He loved football and we would go to any home game in London"

Max must have looked a bit dubious because Cass then preceded to recount half a dozen football chants which brought blushes and plenty of head shaking to a nearby table of what Max guessed were Canadians. He still had not got used to being in a foreign country that had no American tourists.

The food arrived and they chatted more about football and Cass's hometown a stone's throw away from the West Bank. Max had that knack of being a great listener and adding just enough to a conversation that company felt he was fully involved but afterwards found they had learnt very little about the big man. He signalled to the waiter for the bill in the time honoured tradition of waving his hand in the in the shape of a wild signature.

'It may look stupid but it works' he thought. It was as the waiter walked towards him that he saw the glint of metal under the tray. It was way too big to be a pen and the waiter had a distinctly focussed look on his face.

He had six seconds before he reached the table and they were over in a blur but to Max they seemed like they went on for ages.

One and two he spent flicking his eyes around the room and picked up on the fact that there were at least ten sets of eyes trained on their table. Yes he was an interesting sight in his cream suit but not that bloody fascinating.

Three was largely wasted as the 'run' option was raised and immediately dismissed.

Four and his covered the rest of the scene, down - the floor - and then up to the stunning glass dome.

Five and his pistol was out and pointing towards the sky.

Six was an interesting second because two things happened. The waiter got within six feet of the table and was lowering his tray to reveal a semi-automatic pistol. At that point Max's gun thundered a bullet straight up within an inch or so of his own face.

As the waiter recoiled Max leant forward and pushed Cass hard in the chest sending her careering backwards and underneath the adjacent table. Her head reached its safety a slit second before the thousands of pieces of glass from the shattered dome engulfed the dozen tables in the centre of the restaurant.

From that moment it was chaos. Although the domes central panels had long been replaced by safety glass the force of the bullet had created a domino effect and apart from a few small panels at the sides the whole ceiling caved in. Max felt the full force of the falling glass on his back and the back of his head and was probably not far away from being knocked out. The waiter wasn't so lucky as he had instinctively looked to the source of the noise and took the glass in the face. Cass leapt to her feet and grabbed Max's arm. It took a moment for him to respond but within half a minute they were out of the side entrance of the restaurant. Two of Martinez's men were right behind them. That number could very easily have been worse as there had been a total of nine in the restaurant. Mostly at nearby tables. Martinez knew full well that Cass had earned her reputation and despite protests from his men had insisted that all available be involved. He would not be pleased to be proved right but would no doubt have been amazed by the real reason that only a couple of his men were now pursuing Cass through the narrow streets of Old Havana. Sure, Max had created the diversion but he was stumbling along the road almost being pulled along by Cass. She spun Max into a doorway and turning with her gun aloft sent half a dozen shots back in the direction of the two men who dived for cover. Max shook his head and steadied himself against the doorframe. Cass held the gun tight as she reached into the strapping on her left thigh, removed a new clip and swapped it for the spent one in an effortless movement.

"You okay Max?" she shouted.

"Been better" he replied and took up a position on her right shoulder.

"They are about a hundred yards down the street. One behind the corner and the other on the far side of that blue car"

Max looked past her but could not see either man. 'They'll keep under cover if they know what's good for them' he thought. Glancing back he saw a small road with what looked like a market sprawling into it about fifty yards down its length. Max motioned to Cass and she nodded. Still no movement but the unmistakable sound of sirens made the decision for them.

Three bullets rattled into the stonework at the end of the narrow street but Cass and Max were already within yards of the throng of the market. Martinez's men hesitated as they reached the edge of the market and the larger of the two veered off to the left, which unfortunately for them was the opposite to Cass and Max who were making their way quickly towards the railway station.

They ran into the main terminal building and Cass made a beeline for a train that was just leaving the third platform. Max was having great difficulty keeping up and when he clambered aboard the train he was four carriages behind Cass. They made their way towards each other through the crowded cars but there were so many people that it wasn't until the third stop that they reached the same car.

35

"Send a bunch of peasants to do a man's job!"

Martinez screamed at the six of his men that had made it out of the restaurant. The other three were among the large group of people ferried to the state hospital.

"One hundred thousand dollars to the man that finishes this, and I mean FINISH!" he slammed his fist on the table and sent his wine glass over the edge. As the glass hit the ground and shattered the six men in front of him winced.

36

Max laid eyes on Cass and without thinking gave her a huge hug. No sooner had he wrapped his arms around her he let her go and smiled awkwardly. Cass's face carried a frown that quickly turned into a grin.

"You are a very dangerous man to be around" she laughed as they stepped out onto the small open area in between the cars.

"I don't look for it. Honest"

"Nevertheless, it seems to find you" Cass added.

"That wasn't Langustos men. I'm sure I recognised one of them but I can't place him"

"How many of them were there?"

"At least five, but I didn't get a good look on account of someone pushing me under a table"

"Well excuse me" Max replied

"Oh, don't get me wrong. I'm pretty pleased you did. I got a bit of the ceiling in my left leg" she lifted her dress to reveal a two inch gash in what Max admitted was a tanned shapely thigh.

"I was lucky" Max replied feeling the back of his head and finding a raft of bruises and pulling a face.

"Let me look at that" Cass grabbed his hand and for a moment they paused. Hand in hand with the beautiful Cuban countryside rolling by and then her hand moved to his head and she was behind him.

"No harm done. Bruises and cuts but you'll live, again"

"You said that with a hint of the inevitable" Max said as he turned back to face her.

"I have a funny feeling you're pretty good at it" Cass replied and reached inside her waistband and removed a tiny mobile phone which she punched a few numbers into. She raised the phone to her ear and after a few moments rattled of a series of instructions which, as they weren't in English Max couldn't understand.

As she put the phone away the train pulled into the next station and Cass jumped onto the gravel. Max followed and sent plumes of dust into the air as he landed heavily.

'Not exactly Mr.Stealth' Cass thought and headed for the small group of taxis huddled under the limited shade at the front of the station.

37

Eight weeks locked in the confined space had taken its toll on Pete and he could have easily passed himself off as a hunger striker. He looked more gaunt than a catwalk model, well perhaps not that bad. There had been no physical cruelty since his captors had decided that he had nothing interesting to reveal. They had not got far into their repertoire of methods of making people talk before they realised he knew nothing. The broken fingers were healing nicely but he wondered how his typing speed would be affected.

"I'll never be able to play the piano again," he said out loud and the guard outside shouted for him to shut his fascist pig mouth. 'Charming' Pete thought and added in a whisper. "Not that I knew how to play the f'ing piano before anyway!" and immediately chided himself for the use of the cliché. This had gone well past just a good story and he was beginning to wonder if he would ever get out.

38

There were twenty-seven men in total on the quiet airbase in Northern France. Charlotte was a small town about a hundred miles from Normandy whose history was steeped in things military. In the Second World War it had been a regional headquarters for the resistance. The picturesque town square and seventeenth century church held plenty of stories. Tonight, however, Charlotte's place in history would be marked for a very different reason.

In the centre of the airfield were two concrete hangars. They were large enough to have a dozen or so small aircraft but very plain and un-inspirational to the external observer. The tower was nothing special either. Four of the men were in there, a further eleven around the perimeter, two inside the hangars and ten asleep.

There were just eight in the 4x4 by the south gate of the airfield. Eight against seventeen awake. They had spent the previous day and night watching and recording every move and pattern since the planes arrived. They had come in the dusk and at first Durant had only counted three. It had been a painstaking five minutes until the fourth had arrived. He was relieved his information was good. It had been out though on the number of troops at the airfield. He had been told forty, but was pleased his contact had over cooked it.

'The key to the operation was speed and stealth' he reminded himself. He prided himself in ten years of stealing military hardware he had not lost a single one of his men. True, they had not taken anything anywhere near like this before. He flipped his night-vision glasses over his eyes and glanced around his men. They all looked composed, but he knew the adrenaline was pumping through their veins.

"Remember gentlemen, I have no desire to rise higher on Interpol's list because one of you is careless. Lets do it"

He checked his watch.
"0-2:00, mark"

As his watch emitted a small beep the 4x4 rolled through the small gate and towards the back of the unused hangar. No lights and a muffled engine.

39

"I really don't like this," said Colonel Letract as he paced up and down in the command trailer. "That's my men in there," he said pointing at one of the bank of video screens on the desk.

"You know the importance of this mission Colonel" Agent Baber was annoyed at the interruption but had little sympathy for the man. The radio operator at the controls raised his arm and spoke softly into the microphone hooked around his head.

"Subjects have just passed through the perimeter fence"

40

They reached the hangar in a little under a minute and Durant opened the back doors. They filed out two by two and six of them made their way around to the South of the building. The largest of the bunch, a stern faced German called Mantz headed towards the tower. The small Frenchman went straight towards the main building.

Mantz reached the base of the tower and as he did so one of the soldiers emerged with cigarette and lighter in his hands. Still running Mantz raised his pistol and the soldier hit the wall and fell forward crushing his cigarette under his chest. Six more steps and Mantz was inside. He checked his watch. Forty-five seconds before 2:03. He took the grenade from his belt and checked the pin. He tried not to think what he would do if another came down the small staircase. He regretted having to shoot the first one but you couldn't plan for everything.

The Frenchman was standing outside the dormitory and took a moment to peer through the small pane of glass. Thirty seconds to go. Four of the team were now by the open doors of the main hangar and they could see all eight of the men inside. They were working on one of the planes and Durant cursed under his breath.

'I really hope that it's a service' he thought. They had got this far and the last thing they needed was for one of the planes to be in pieces. Fifteen seconds.

The last two had set up the scrambling unit. It was extremely heavy and they were thankful that the unused hangar had a large sturdy table in the office. They had taken the precaution of putting the unit down as they entered which had proved to be a good move as there were two guards inside. Fairly vicious blows to the head and they had been taken care of and were bundled into a corner of the office. They completed the initiation sequence that would bathe a five-mile radius in radar static. Five seconds.

41

Baber was watching the monitor trained on the tower as the grenades went off. At precisely three minutes past two the hangar, main building and tower were a mass of smoke. The force of the blast in the tower caved two of the windows that drew a sharp intake of breath from Baber.

"Shit!" he said quietly as the four men in the trailer were glued to their screens.

Colonel Letract headed for the door but Baber signalled to his burly colleague who blocked the way.

'Get out of my way!" the Colonel snapped, but the man in the dark suit made no movement.

"You know we have to let this run its course" Baber said without emotion. Inside he was worried though. He knew that this was a make or break situation for him. Not only had both the British Defence Minister and Home Secretary been involved in the briefing, but both had expressed grave concerns. Not for the planes as they were due to be decommissioned in a few years anyway, but for the NATO troops involved. If it ever got out that the British had sanctioned this then the consequences could be dire. Most of the men stationed at Charlotte were French, naturally, but four were Italians, four British and a Norwegian.

42

The eight men moved quickly in the hangar. After a brief check that no soldiers had made it past the gas, they had converged on the planes and paired off two to each aircraft. Durant took a moment to smile to himself.

'We're actually going to do this'

He placed a hand on the cold grey steel of the wing. His partner was checking the wiring underneath the panel that had been open when they came in and signalled that everything was ok. He bolted the panel down and they got into the cockpit.

The unexpected delay had cost them four of the five minutes he had set aside. The engines roared into life one by one and they rolled out onto the runway. There were no runway lights to guide them but the four pilots were experienced enough not to need them. The blue and orange flames of the jet engines erupted and the first jet soared into the air closely followed by the second and the third. Durant looked back at the hangar as they taxied onto the runway. The helmet giving him a steady flow of oxygen limited his vision.

'Four Tornadoes' he thought 'and clean once again' he smiled as the force of the takeoff pinned him back into his seat.

43

Baber had never met the deputy director of MI5 other than at social functions. Claire Wilson was the youngest woman to have risen to her current grade in the secret service and many tipped her to take the top job in the next five years. She was thirty-eight, tall athletic and had worked her way through a number of tough consular assignments. These included stints in Kosho, Zaire and Northern Ireland. It was widely known that she had a thorough knowledge of ballistics that formed part of her major at MIT and post-grad at Harvard. It was also know that she despised tardiness and Baber had been a good fifteen minutes early for their meeting, despite his office being in the adjacent building. He had been sitting in one of the huge brown leather armchairs opposite her desk for five minutes before she looked up from the files on her desk and removed her gold rimmed glasses.

"In your own words, Mr.Baber, perhaps you would like to precee the operation of two nights ago"

Baber straightened slightly in his chair and in a flat tone said.

"Operation 129A was completed successfully. Four RAF Tornado aircraft, known to be sought by the Langusto arms syndicate were stolen from the Charolotte airfield at shortly after 2am and are currently thought to be en route to Qatar"

"Currently thought?" Wilson raised an eyebrow.
"I take it from your choice of words and the lack of contrary information in my files that you don't have a fix on the aircraft at the present time?"

"No Ma'am" Baber answered and had he been able to show any emotion he would have been grimacing.

"Well" she paused
"Let me give you the feedback I received from the Home Secretary this morning" Wilson stood up clutching a large file and started walking around the room.

"Twenty four men admitted to hospital with severe smoke burns, five of whom are still in there. Two concussions and, as you are probably aware, one young Frenchman with gunshot wounds. The vest he was wearing saved his life but looks unlikely to have saved his right arm.

Baber stayed silent. He had heard about the wounded man immediately after the raid. Colonel Letract had ensured Baber watched as they loaded him into the field ambulance. His Kelvar vest had done its job with the first bullet but the second had hit him in the shoulder. Baber had felt numb as they had carried the young man on a stretcher. He wouldn't have gone through with the operation if it hadn't been for Durant. It was so out of character for Durant's men to use their weapons. Stun guns were the traditional tools he used and the reason Baber's team had engineered for the information on the whereabouts of the planes to be leaked to Durant's right hand man in Milan.

'Maybe he had difficulty getting a team together at short notice'

"And you view this as successful?"

Wilson snapped. Baber took this as a rhetorical question and was relieved when she continued.

"Thirty million pounds worth of aircraft and you are gambling this on this Jones gentlemen? I've read the file Mr.Baber and I'm rather surprised you got this through." Baber winced. He'd cut a few corners, no wait, a lot of corners, and pulled in all his outstanding favours to make this happen.

"The question is can you trust this man to follow through?"

She had both her hands face down on the desk and was staring right into Baber's eyes.

"I'd stake my reputation on it" he replied in a confident tone.

"Oh, don't worry Mr.Baber" she smiled.

"You already have"

44

Max was having trouble sleeping. Being shot at by Cuban thugs had that effect on him. He was safely back in his suite at the Grande. Cass had assured him that as it was the Langustos' territory, Martinez's men would stay well clear. He wasn't sure but he was beginning to get the feeling that he would have great difficulty not paying attention to her. His mind was just starting to drift to thoughts of her three floors beneath him when his PDA began beeping in the living room.

He swung his legs over the side of the bed and reached for his robe. He fastened it around his waist and sat down on the sofa. He reached into his open briefcase and flipped open the PDA.

B: Max?

M: Hi. Do you realise that it's 3am here?

B: Sorry. We have a situation.

M: Where's Easton?

B: Easton's not on the call. It's a little delicate.

M: Hold on. Easton's running this little show?

B: Technically, yes.

M: Technically?

B: Technically. This doesn't concern him.

M: Well it concerns me. What's going on?

B: We've lost the Tornadoes.

M: Wasn't that the general idea?

B: No, I mean we really lost them. We were all set to track them across Europe but we lost them somewhere over Finland.

Max looked at the screen and began typing a reply. He stopped and held down the delete key. This was not good, definitely not good.

B: Max?

M: Yeah I'm here. If anything surfaces this end I'll let you know.

He clicked the enter button. He had a really bad feeling about this.

45

Cass's hair was still wet from the shower when the phone rang. She instinctively drew her pistol from its holster lying on the bed and stood with her back to the wall before lifting the receiver. It was one of the first things they had been taught - if you want to attack someone, get someone to phone them. As well as distracting it also telegraphs where they are in the room (unless they have a cordless) and means at least one of their hands is occupied.

"Si?" she answered.

"Ah Bueno" said the hoarse voice on the other end.

"Itsa Uncle Guiseppe. How's about that breakfast?"

Cass grinned at Max's awful accent.

"Si. Fifteen minutes" she replied. He was early, but nothing this big man did surprised her. She dressed in a plain white blouse and slacks and sprayed some L'eau Dissey perfume on her neck. She realised she was standing in front of the mirror fiddling with her hair and she shook her head for a moment regretting having cut those long brown locks.

46

"Hey its 'Our Man in Havana" Max tried to sound enthusiastic. In the first two weeks he had met with Tremiere twice and talked with him on the phone a dozen times with little result.

"What you got for me?" he asked.

"We think we've found the last place he stayed in Havana"

He certainly had Max's attention.

"Where" Max asked.

"It's a flea pit of a hotel downtown. We're pretty sure it was him. The manager of the hotel gave us a good description.

"How on earth did you find it?" Max was curious.

"To be honest" Tremiere sounded a little embarrassed.

"A little bit of luck. One of our contacts picked up a small time pickpocket using one of Pete's credit cards. He had claimed he found it in the trash so we did a door to door check of the hotels in the area"

Max didn't particularly like Tremiere but was thankful for the lead.

"Hey Tremiere, thanks"

"No Problem Mr.Jones"

Max put the phone down and wondered whether he should tell Cass. He had about two hours before he was due at the Langustos for dinner.

'I'll just take a little look' he thought and put on his jacket.

47

The taxi was a Lada and Max had found it about two streets down from the hotel. He doubted the Langustos were having him followed, but it never hurt to be sure. He was right though. The manager of the Grande was keeping Allesandro up to date with his comings and goings but the Langusto family had too much going on domestically to waste the manpower. Despite Luco's cousin's influence in the Police Force, there was a marked increase in the police activity in Havana. Income from their loan-sharking operations was down 30% and Allesandro knew that the other families were being hit as hard. The focus on drugs was hitting Martinez hard, followed by prostitution, which hit everybody. Max hadn't seen evidence of either, not that he had been paying much attention.

The taxi pulled in front of a grey building that was identical to the dozen or so others on that street. Max handed the driver a five-dollar bill and stepped out. The words 'Hotel' and

'Vacancy' were barely readable from the sidewalk they were so small. 'So much for Marketing' Max smiled.

The six crumbling steps led to a heavy set panelled door with two long panes of glass. Both were cracked and dirty and Max closed the door behind him carefully. The "reception" was a small hatch in the wall and what Max assumed was the manager sat glued to a small black and white portable TV on the back counter. He had his face pointed away from Max and every couple of seconds emitted a small chuckle. There was an episode of the Three Stooges that had been dubbed in Spanish, badly. Max rang the little bell and the man turned his head slightly so he could see Max out of the corner of his eye.

"Yes?" the man said as if getting an answer was the last thing on his mind. Max held up a twenty dollar bill and that seemed to be enough to get his interest. Max reached into his breast pocket and retrieved a fifty. At this the man got up from his seat and came to the counter.

"Ok, Ok. What kind of girl do you want? I can get big, little, black, white, Asian. You like fat? I got fat womens too" the little man grinned. Max wondered if this little man who was all of five feet tall would be suspicious if he didn't play along.

"I like BIG women" Max laughed.

"and give me room eight". Before the man could answer he added "My lucky number" and laughed. The little man grinned and took both of the bills.

"One hour" he said in an excited tone.

"Okey dokey?" he added.

"Okey dokey" said Max and took the key.

There was no lift and Max noticed that the door to the fire escape on the second floor had a padlock on it. The corridor was dim due to only one of the light fittings being on. It was an overstatement to call it a fitting - 'wire with a bulb' would be more accurate.

The lock on the door of room 8 was set very low in the frame and Max had to bend to get to it. He saw that it was the fifth location of the lock and guessed that there was more plastic wood than real wood left in the door. The room itself was sparse and had a dreary layout with a bed, a small wardrobe without a door and a chest of drawers with two missing drawers – a chest of drawer in fact. The curtains were a nasty bottle green but still competed for the most pleasant feature of the room, closely followed by a cigarette stained coffee table. Max closed the door and began to search the room. It didn't take long and he was beginning to think that he had wasted his time when he got to the waste-bin. It was almost empty but had a few scraps of paper in the bottom. Max carefully took them out and unfolded them onto the table. He recognised Pete's handwriting straight away and felt a pang of excitement. There were two pieces of what appeared to be a list of notes. Max laid them together and grabbed a pen and pad from his jacket and copied over the words.

MARTINEZ

DRUGS FUNDS ARMS

HAVANA – COLUMBIA

VARADERO

BACARDI?

Max looked at the page in the notebook.

'Bloody shorthand' he thought and wondered what Pete meant.

At that moment the door opened and Max leapt to his feet.

'Ola senor' said the woman that filled the doorway (literally). Max was a little stunned. Whilst the woman was pretty short, that was the only dimension in which she was lacking. Wearing a skin-tight dress Max guessed that she would qualify as having a circumference. As she stepped into the room her huge bosom bounced wildly and Max was reminded of the bouncy castle his brother had hired for his nephew's fifth birthday party last summer. She shut the door with her bottom and it shook heavily – the door not the bottom. Well, actually, the bottom as well.

"You like?" she asked as she gave Max a Meringue shake. For one of the first times in a long time Max was speechless. He immediately thought of the padlock on the fire escape door and took half a step backward and glanced out of the window. The roof of the adjoining building was about ten feet away and fifteen feet down. He shuffled over to the other side of the room and the woman grinned.

"Shy boy, shy boy" she laughed and retrieved the door key Max had left on top of the chest of drawer and locked the door. Max raised his hand in protest and she laughed again. He stepped forward and reached for the key but she quickly slipped it into her large cleavage, wagged a large stubby finger at him and shook her head. Max looked at her arms and calculated that although there was enough flesh on them for a dozen supermodels, he didn't rate his chances against them.

He raised his palms in submission and pointed to the bed. The woman giggled and rolled onto the bed and hitched up her dress. Max seized his chance as her bulk was obscuring her view, but he knew he only had a few seconds. He grabbed the window and slid it up and was straight out onto the ledge. He looked at the roof below which now seemed miles away, and he hesitated.

"Senor?" the woman called from the bed. A mental picture of his head being crushed in between those huge thighs was enough to inspire him and Max leapt across the gap and the dark street below.

He landed in a heap on the roof and rolled to a stop. He felt his right shoulder where the wound screamed out at him. He reached down and immediately realised he had ripped a few of the stitches and blood was seeping out onto his cream shirt.

"Damn" he said under his breath and struggled to his feet.

48

An empty Tornado weighs 14,500kg, which generally means they aren't the easiest things to move around. The simplest way to transport them is to fly them to their destination, but that option is also fraught with problems. You need a good pilot, no scratch that, you need a bloody good pilot. Why? Apart from the fact that this is a pretty powerful piece of aeronautical engineering, it's also nicked which means that you need to be able to fly it below conventional airspace or it will inevitably get caught on radar. And what don't you want to do if you are dealing in stolen fighter planes? Get caught on radar. Colonel Riley was just that type of pilot. He was just about old enough to have seen action in the Gulf War and until two years ago he would have gladly given his life for his country. The thought of flying along a few hundred feet off the ground heading for an abandoned airstrip in Northern Qatar in a stolen plane would have disgusted him. Charles Riley was a patriot through and through but he had one little problem. Well, about two hundred and fifty thousand little problems to be precise. His weakness for Tequila and gambling combined had left him in debt to a loan Shark in Philadelphia and he was pretty desperate. His wife had cleaned him out after she found him having sex on their sofa with their son's primary school teacher. Well, she was cute. She had taken the house and their savings and he was just left with his Mustang. Not that that wasn't enough of get him a string of women in the six months since they separated. A second youth and he had been determined to enjoy it. Its just that he enjoyed it too much and the day he found himself on the floor of his apartment with a broken nose lying in a pool of his own vomit after a visit from his creditors he knew he had to find a fast way out. As he brought the Tornado around and lined up with the dusty runway he told himself that he only had a few more trips to do and he would be free.

49

Cass opened her hotel room door cautiously with her pistol at her side. She relaxed when she saw that Max was alone and ushered him in.

"You're early again," she said as she walked back across her room towards the bathroom.

"I'll be a little while yet," she added as she leaned over for her hairdryer. She was wearing a thick hotel dressing gown and her long dark legs were glistening. Max saw he black dress hanging on the wardrobe door on a hanger and let out a quiet whistle. He could picture what she would look like in it. He forced himself back to the present.

"Hey Cass. We have a few problems," he said loudly and she stopped drying and came out of the bathroom.

"What was that?" she said.

Max sat down in one of the armchairs and Cass sat in the other.

"You know these arms that I'm supposed to be buying from the Langustos?"

"Yes" she said and began combing her hair

"You know I said that it was, err, quite a large shipment?"

"Come on Max, you know you don't have to tell me the details" she laughed. "you know I would have to report it back and your government wouldn't be too keen on that"

Max nodded.

"I know. But I need your help and you can't do that unless you know more"

Cass put the comb down.

"Okay, but you know the rules"

Max nodded again. He told her about the Tornadoes and how they had lost them. He had her full attention and when he finished her eyes were wide and she sat back in her seat.

"Shit." She said. "I bet MI5 are pissed"

"Understatement" Max said

"So what can we do?" she asked.

"We need to find out where the planes are being stored"

"Oh, just that" she laughed. "And has the wonderful London got any ideas how the hell you are supposed to do that?"

"I've been told to get the information to them by Friday. Three days. I figured I would try and get it in casual conversation with Luco on the golf course tomorrow"

"Sure he's really going to let that slip," she said with a heavy dose of sarcasm. "Don't kid yourself Max. These guys don't mess about. I still can't believe you guys lost the planes. We'd never do that"

"Ah, but would you have done it in the first place?" Max snapped. He didn't know why he was being so defensive.

"Probably not" she conceded.

"We'll just have to get the information tonight. I've got the blueprints of the house and we can narrow it down to one of their studies"

"One of?" Max asked.

"Yes. Luco and Allesandro both have their own studies on separate sides of the house".

"Two studies, two of us, no problem" Max laughed.

Cass gave him a mock sneer and got up to go to the bathroom. She stopped and turned back.

"What was the other problem?" she asked.

"You got a needle and thread?"

Cass put her hands on her hips and grinned.

"Why, you lost a button?"

"Err, not exactly" Max grimaced as he took of his jacket and revealed his blood stained shirt.

"How on earth did you do that?" Cass exclaimed and helped Max remove his shirt.

"Oh, it's an old war wound" he said as Cass reached into one of the drawers and took out a fresh towel.

"And this?" she asked pointing to the heavy bruising around his shoulder and side.

"Fell out of a window" Max smiled and winced as Cass splashed some Iodine from a brown bottle she had taken from her vanity case.

"Ouch, that stings" Max said.

"Good" she snapped.

He could sense she was annoyed that he had gone off by himself.

"I hope it was worth it," she said as she finished cleaning the wound.

"Not really" he replied and he retrieved the notepad and passed it to her.

"It's from Pete's hotel room" he explained. She looked at the words.

"Drugs funds arms" she read.

"That figures. We always had Martinez down as a player. The Langustos stay away from drugs, they leave that to Martinez. The connection with Columbia is interesting. I'll run that one back to Tel Aviv and see what comes up".

"What do you think he means by Varadero and Bacardi?" Max asked.

"Maybe it's a name of a hotel in Varadero" she suggested.

"Nope. Tried that. Our boys are working on it though" he said and tried to look hopeful.

50

He was pushed roughly into the chair and he felt the rope burns into his wrists as his hands were lashed to the arms of the chair. He tried again to open his eyes but the light was still too bright and pointed straight at his face.

"Who are you?"

"Who do you work for?"

The same questions over and over punctuated only by a punch in the ribs or a slap around the face. His answers were mumbled for his jaw was swollen and his lips cracked in a number of places. He could taste blood again and found he couldn't swallow.

"Water?" he asked quietly.

"Agua?" laughed the burly man behind the light.

"But of course Senor" and a glass of cold water was held up to Pete's mouth. He guzzled at the cold liquid but almost immediately spluttered and shook violently. The chair toppled and his head hit the floor with a thud. Salt and lemon juice. 'Bastards' he thought as they left him lying on the floor. He had told them the truth on the second day but they had not believed him. Their paranoia combined with the fact that all Pete's identification had been made to look like he was a research assistant for a horticultural institute made for a difficult to credit story. Most of the questioning centred on the Cuban authorities that of course Pete knew relatively little about. Two men grabbed the chair and set it straight again.

"Now" said the same voice.

"Let's try that again".

51

Cass and Max walked out of the front doors of the Grande arm in arm and were greeted by the black shiny Cadillac and the two henchmen Max had spent the day with at the military facility.

'Hello again boys' Cass thought. As she got into the back seat. She wondered if they had found the tracking device she had used and sat back in the leather seat and smiled.

Oh they had found it all right. Or rather, the head of security at the house had found it. It had set off one of the sensors when they had taken it into the garage that had been converted into a carwash. They had both been penalised a month's wages and security at the house had been stepped up.

The route out to the Langustos was very beautiful at night. The lights of Havana drifted away in the background with the dark hills and the infrequent lights of the houses dotted by the roadside. The two in the front didn't say a word and Max was uptight. He wanted to talk to Cass and could feel her arm linked into his but apart from a few smiles the trip passed by without incident.

The house was more impressive than Cass had imagined. The plans didn't do it justice. Four towers, one at each corner with a central pointed roof with a smooth white dome. They passed through the gates and Cass felt uneasy and somehow naked without her guns. Max got out and opened the door for her and she stepped out, the gravel crunching under her heels. Luco Langusto was standing at the top of the steps and extended a hand and friendly grin.

"János" he beamed.

"And?"

"Oh, this is Katherine Derrick" Max smiled and held Cass's hand as she walked up the steps.

"Charmed" said Luco and lightly kissed her outstretched hand.

"You old dog" Luco whispered into Max's ear.

"Where did you find her?" he asked.

"Wife of a Venezuelan oil baron" Max grinned.

"Met her in a bar. Husband is hopping around the islands on business apparently". He nudged Luco on the arm as Cass stopped at the entrance to the Veranda.

"Katherine, this is Allesandro and Emilio" Max introduced her two the two men who had risen as she approached. She put on her best smile but she struggled to hide her disgust. She knew Allesandro Langusto. She had seen his work first hand in Tel Aviv, in Penang, in Hong Kong.

'Oh how I wish I had my Sig now you oily little bastard' she thought.

She realised she was pausing a little too long with her greeting and took a step towards the bar.

Allesandro stepped forward and offered a drink and Max and Cass perched on the tall bamboo bar stools and surveyed the long mirrored bar.

"Mai Tai" Cass purred and stroked Max's arm.

"Oburn single malt if you have it" Max added.

The barman mixed Cass's drink and as he was pouring it into a large glass with some fresh mint she noticed something odd behind the bar. She didn't have long to dwell on it though as Luco asked her a question.

"So Katherine, what brings you to Havana?"

She picked up her drink and as they walked across to one of the tables she replied.

"Oh, some tedious business" she said demurely.

"But I'm succeeding in finding things to keep me amused" she smiled and threw a glance at Max. Luco grinned and looked at Max.

'You lucky bastard' he thought.

52

Dinner was a lavish affair of six courses and contrary to everything Max had heard and experienced of Cuba's limited cuisine. It was 95% imported of course. The Langustos spent a small fortune on food. Allesandro's wife Maria had trained as a restranteur and their chef was one of the best in Havana. They had closed the restaurant for the evening and half of the staff were up at the house.

The meal finished and Maria, a striking dark-skinned woman five years younger than her husband, offered to take Cass on a tour of the house while the men headed for the billiard room for brandy and cigars. Max hadn't smoked for about fifteen years and the taste of the world's finest cigars was nothing short of heaven.

"So, how progresses my purchase?" Max asked.

"Manjana János. It is all in hand. We are in fact ahead of schedule. The merchandise will be in Qatar by Sunday" Luco replied.

Max tried not to show his panic.

"Sunday?" he asked. "I will call Klaus and move everything forward to Monday".

Luco and Allesandro exchanged satisfied looks.

That left Max just four days to find Pete. He would lose tomorrow afternoon playing golf with Luco, which meant three days.

53

"And this is the eastern tower" Maria used a sweeping arm motion as she led Cass into the base of the tower. Identical to the other three except this time they climbed the stairs to the second floor.

"János tells me you have a wonderful library," Cass said as they reached the landing. She had done her homework and Maria's eyes lit up at the mention of her great passion. She collected classic novels and over the years her hobby had cost Allesandro a lot of money. Even with his income and lavish tastes he had balked when she had spent £20,000 on a Dickens first edition at Sotheby's.

The library doubled as Allesandro's office and Cass pretended to be looking the other way as Maria keyed in the security code by the door. 342632. His wife's measurements at a guess. The office was decadently done out in walnut. No veneer here. The desk was the size of a table tennis table and three of the four walls were covered from floor to ceiling with books. The bay window overlooked the canyon and the veranda and in the middle of the bay stood a magnificent wooden globe.

"This is a complete set of the works of Beatrix Potter" Maria lifted the delicate works from the shelf onto the desk. Cass kept smiling and giving words of encouragement. "Beautiful", "Magical", "Stunning". Maria was in her element and Cass had about twenty minutes to case the room. The desk had huge drawers that weren't locked. Maria had slid one of them open to get a pen to note down a few of Cass's suggestions for additions to her collection.

54

When they rejoined the men they were playing poker in the lounge. There was a bottle of Courvoisier on the table, which was nearly empty, and Cass wondered if that was the same one that was full just two hours before. It was just five of them left now and Max was looking very worse for wear.

"Ah Katherine, you've come to save me from these scoundrels" Max grinned.

"I hardly think you are in a position to call these darling gentlemen scoundrels" she twinkled.

"You however, will go severely down in my estimations if you don't get me back to my hotel.

Marco shook his head and tutted.

"Bad Kovács" he laughed and Max grinned.

"I have my orders gentlemen" he got up and headed towards the door with Cass on his arm.

"I'll see you at the club at two" he shouted over his shoulder and Luco waved a hand.

"Si, Si. Two o'clock" he called back.

55

The same car and men took them back to the Grande and Max wondered whether they had been standing outside waiting the whole time. The journey back was just as quiet. Cass's mind was racing. She was sure there was something in that office that would incriminate the Langustos. Max was asleep. Scotch, wine brandy and the heat once they had left the air-conditioning of the house had knocked him out. He awoke as they came to a stop in front of the hotel.

The manager winked at Max as they walked across the lobby and got into the lift. As the doors closed Max whispered.
"Nice act"
"My life is an act" Cass forced a smile and steadied Max as he stumbled.

They reached the 21st floor and Max fiddled with the key to his room.

"Why don't you stay?" he asked, surprising himself with his boldness.

"Okay" she said simply and walked over to the wardrobe and retrieved one of Max's large T-shirts. Her dress slid off her shoulders and she slipped off her bra and clutching the T-shirt went into the bedroom. She smiled as she saw that Max was face down on the bed snoring quietly. She looked at him sprawled on the bed and warned herself that this wasn't a good idea. She managed, with some difficulty to get Max's clothes off and under the sheets. She put her arms around his big frame. Murmurs of contentment came from his side of the bed and for the first time in years Cassandra Yillette slept through the night.

56

Max wasn't sure where he was but he was sure he hadn't invited the family of kangaroos that had taken up residence inside his skull. He counted his limbs and found he had three arms. Closer examination revealed that the third was not his, and came with a head of black hair which was resting on his stomach. His head was really pounding. He tried to move his arm a little and the head of hair became a flash and he found himself with the barrel of a pistol shoved up his nose.

"Oh Max, I'm sorry" Cass said as she hastily removed the gun and placed it on the nightstand.

"Good morning to you too" Max said trying to lighten the mood.

"I guess I'm used to sleeping alone" she said sheepishly. Max had no idea how Cass had ended up in his bed, but he was extremely happy about it nonetheless.

"I'll order some breakfast" she smiled and headed for the lounge. Max gingerly rose and sat on the side of the bed. He looked down and saw that he had a pair of South Park boxers on. They must have been in the pocket of his suitcase and the maid must have unpacked them when he arrived. His brother had given them to him for his fortieth birthday. The cartoon face of Cartman was looking up at him telling him to "Respect My Authoritah" in large yellow letters.

"Oh by the way" Cass shouted from the shower.

"Nice Pants!"

57

Durant knew why he was anxious. He had five million reasons to be precise. That was his share after the team had been paid. He would retire on this one. He had said that before, but his decision had been made for him after the de-brief and Mantz's admission that he had popped one of the soldiers. He would be way up the wanted list by now. That stupid pig. Ten years and no casualties and he has to go and shoot someone. The Cubans had confirmed the exchange would take place on Monday and by Tuesday morning he would be the new owner of a little town nobody had heard of on the coast of Brazil.

58

Max mixed two sachets of Resolve into his orange juice and used it to wash down a couple more Ibuprofen. Cass was already halfway through her eggs and was reading the front page of the Havana Times.

"I got a fantastic look around Allesandro's office last night"

"You did?" Max replied glad that the awkward silence had been broken.

"Yeah. I'll try and get back in there when we go back for dinner again in a couple of days. I, must admit I'm looking forward to the golf tomorrow".

"You joining us?" Max asked surprised.

"Thought I might" Cass smiled. "Played a little when I was at university".

"Is there nothing that the lady cannot do" Max smiled and braved a mouthful of egg.

"Drink quite as heavily as you?" she grinned.

"Cheap shot" he said and pretended to sulk.

"Did you notice something at the bar last night?"

Cass asked.

"The twenty different types of Scotch?"

"No. There was a bank of bottles with their labels removed. Clear spirit, vodka or something"

"That's weird" Max agreed. "Wouldn't have thought they were into home brew"

"No they had branded bottle tops"

"What brand?"

"Don't know. It was some kind of a crest"

Max grabbed a pen and a sheet of hotel notepaper. Cass drew the crest and handed it to Max.

"Used to be a barman me" he added a few more lines.

"BACARDI" he wrote below the crest.

Cass jumped up and shouted as she reached the door.

"Back in a minute".

When she got back from her room she had a set of briefing notes which weren't a lot of use to Max as they were in Israeli.

"I knew I had seen that somewhere before" she said.

"I'm annoyed I didn't pick up on it in Pete's notes. The Martinez family runs part of the small island of Bacardi not far from the Dominican Republic. The rivalry between the two families is such that all references to the Martinez family are banned"

"You're telling me that is goes as far as taking the labels off bottles of rum?" Max asked.

"Oh yes. Bacardi Island is a big part of the Martinez's history".

Max stood up.

"We've got to get out to that island," he said.

59

By the time Cass and Max drove the two hours out to Varadero and the golf course their itinerary for Friday was set. They had chartered a plane from Havana to Puerto Plata on the Northern Coast of the Dominican Republic. From there a hire car to the town of Cabarete where daily tourist trips went out to the Southern bay of Bacardi Island. They turned off the main road and Max looked at the mansion on the coast ahead of them. Max could see at least five holes with water and made a mental note to get a lot of spare balls. They got their clubs and headed to the first tee where Luco and his caddy were waiting. Luco looked genuinely surprised to see Cass and he smiled.

"I see we have an audience" he laughed and tapped Max on the shoulder.

"No sir" Cass replied in a syrupy voice.

"You have some competition" she raised an eyebrow and reached in the cart and retrieved a three wood. Luco grinned but looked confused. As she walked to the tee she whispered to Luco.

"I have to do something with my days, and I can't abide tennis or horse-riding. I find them both so unladylike".

Luco and Max both stared as Cass smashed her ball down the middle of the fairway. Luco gave her a 'lucky hit' look and Max shrugged his shoulders.

60

Eighteen holes later and they headed back to the clubhouse following behind Luco's cart. Max had got through half a dozen balls – one straight into the ocean on the tenth hole. Luco had lost just three. Cass, however had her original ball in her bag and had taken them by eight shots. Max had been three shots off Luco's score. It would have been much more but for a couple of lucky chips which had rattled into the hole.

"You didn't need to beat him so badly" Max said quietly.

"I know" said Cass "but I enjoyed making him squirm," she said through her teeth.

Luco had come with a stretch Mercedes and Max and Cass made a quick call to the hire car company who agreed for their car to be left at the golf club. It was an interesting ride back to Havana with Luco explaining in detail his family's sugar beet empire for Cass's benefit. He in turn listened to her stories of her husband's oil business and Max decided that not only had the person who had put together Cass's cover had done an excellent job and that she was very, very thorough.

61

They had dinner at the Langustos restaurant and Max wore a sharp dark blue suit with Cass in an ankle length red dress. Max found it difficult to take his eyes off her the whole evening. Once again at the end of the meal the ladies separated off and the men sat in the corner.

"I have another interested party" Max said to Allesandro as he lit his cigar. "although not on the same scale of course" he added.

"Okay" Luco replied. "What's the shopping list?"

"Missiles" Max said.

"Missiles?" said Allesandro.

Max removed the cigar from his mouth and gestured with it.

"That a problem?" he asked.

"No" said Luco quickly "Just a little unusual".

"Unusual is my game" Max smiled.

"Fine. What sort?" he asked firing up his laptop.

"Cruise, anything in that arena"

"How many?"

"Around a hundred"

'At around a $100,000 a piece that's a cool $10m' Allesandro thought.

"Which types were you particularly interested in?"

'Oh Shit' Max thought, 'he's testing me'

"Well, I need to get some SAM surface to air missiles and I would normally go for something like SA11 Gadfly – its got a range of just over 30km and you can get 4 of them on the loader"

"Nice" replied Allessandro. "And how about air-to –surface?"

"AS-18s."

"Oh yes. That's 500kg each".

'Max smiled. He knew what he was trying'

"Well, the warhead is about 320kg but the whole thing weighs around 960kg"

Allesandro smiled. He couldn't resist testing people.

"And for Anti-tank I favour the AT-9s" Max added.

Allessandro grinned and tapped the keyboard.

"So you sure we can't tempt you with something to launch them off?" He turned the laptop around.

Name	Ka-50 Hokum
Type	Attack helicopter
Year	1982
Engine	2 x TV3-117VMA turboshaft, 2x2200hp.
Wingspan	7.34 m
Length	15.6 m (rotors turning)
Height	4.9 m
Rotor	4.9 m
Weight	9800 kg/10800 kg
Max. speed	350 km/h
Op. Range	450 km
Ferry Range	1100 km
Crew	1
Armament	1 x 30 mm gun 2A42 (500 rds),
	12 x Antitank missiles AT-9,
	80 x 80mm or 20 x 122mm Rockets
	AS-10 Anti-radar missiles,
	UPK-23-250 Gun pod,
	GUV-8700 Machine-gun pod

Max smiled.

"No thanks. There's plenty of them knocking around"

Allesandro turned the laptop back and found the full list.

"These are your alternatives".

Easton had taken Max through all the different types of missile that the US authorities were interested in. Max saw all of them on the list.

He made a mental note of each with the stocks.

"I'll confirm on Monday" Max said and turned the screen back. "I think we'll have a deal" he smiled.

62

Max left Cass in her room while he hooked up his PDA to transfer. He opened the dialogue with the missile list and Baber was the first to join two minutes later. Max had wondered why they used the PDAs but Baber had explained that this way their transmissions were encoded and that mobile phones were still too easy to hack into.

B. Nice list Max! Any news on your friend?

M. Have a strong lead but nothing yet. Any luck with those planes?

B. Zero. I gather you got nothing from the Langustos.

M. Not yet. We'll be there Saturday and will try again.

B.What do you mean "we"?

Max cursed himself for the slip.

M. The royal 'we'. They're treating me like royalty.

B. Don't get too excited. If I was spending $50m I'd get treated like The Queen as well.

E. Good evening gentlemen. I'm afraid I have some bad news.

B. What?

E. This operation is officially over. Effective immediately.

B. On whose authority?

E. Don't know. All I know is it's a lot higher than me.

M. Bullshit. You can't just pull the plug.

E. It's over Max.

M. Like hell it is.

B. Max if E says it's over then its over. I'll have Tremiere arrange a flight for you tomorrow.

M. I'm not going anywhere.

B. Don't do this Max. We can't help you out there.

Max typed the words 'Then SCREW YOU' but thought better of it.

M. I'll sort out my own flight tomorrow.

Max flipped the cover over the PDA.

'Why did they have to lose those planes' he thought and threw the PDA hard onto the bed. It bounced off and cluttered into the headboard and split into a number of pieces, two of which fell onto the floor. Max sighed and grabbed the pieces and froze immediately as his eyes caught the word 'detonation'. He placed the three pieces carefully onto the table and ran out of the room.

63

"I'm very impressed," said Cass as she fiddled with the wires with a tiny pair of tweezers. She had a magnifying glass attachment over her right eye and was examining the back of the PDA.

"And its safe is it?" Max asked. There were beads of sweat on his forehead.

"Oh yeah. I've disconnected the power for the moment. Clever little thing. The right command and the timer starts running".

"Let me guess. The command can also be sent remotely?"

"Clever Boy" Cass said and ruffled Max's hair.

"And which side would I be on?" he fumed.

"Max" Cass said solemnly. "Sides don't matter, everyone takes out insurance"

"Remind me to beat the crap out of Baber when I see him next"

"He might not have known. This is a very tidy piece of work. You're rather fortunate you didn't remove this floor of the hotel when you threw this".

Max shuddered. He didn't feel all that lucky.

"I think I can reprogram it to only take a local command"

"Oh Goody" Max said. "Why don't you just trash it?"

"Two good reasons. First, they will get very suspicious if you suddenly go offline and second, it might come in useful."

64

"Macedonia!" Baber's voice was verging on the pleading.

"James, I don't have a lot of choice here. It was that or the Ukraine"

Steve Parkes was Baber's boss and a fairly new breed as MI5 goes. He had been amazed when the Americans canned the operation, but MI5 were the ones that had lost the planes so weren't in too strong a position to argue. Wilson had asked for Baber to be assigned 'As far away as bloody possible'

"You're lucky you're not being suspended" Parkes said sternly.

"You know that's not right" Baber argued.

"You leave on Wednesday. Be ready. I need a full write up on this farce Monday morning"

"Yes sir" replied Baber and headed out of the door.

Parkes didn't say anything to Baber but he wasn't too comfortable with this. He had sensed Wilson wasn't either. Something stank.

65

Puerto Plata was a fair sized airport with a main runway right on top of the sea. The flight from Havana was quick but uncomfortable. Max hated small planes. It had been twenty years since he'd been in a Cessna and had jumped out of that one. To be fair he had thoroughly enjoyed the parachute jump and gone straight back up for another. This wasn't quite Swansea airfield.

The rental 4x4 was waiting for them and as soon as they left the main part of the town Cass double-checked the rear-view mirror.

"We've got a tail," she said calmly.

"Don't turn around" she said quickly as Max went to turn his head.

"We need to lose them before we get to Cabarete" Max said.

"No chance" replied Cass.

"Its one road. We will have to lose them in the town itself"

Max guessed it was Langusto's men and he was sort of correct. The first tail in the black jeep was two of Allesandro's men but the blue car had four of Martinez's men. They had been placed at Havana airport to keep an eye out for Cass and couldn't believe their luck.

Cabarete was not a large town. It consisted of a mile-long beach, a market of sorts and a few dozen interwoven streets lined with stalls selling knock-offs and cheap cigars. Max knew from the Lonely Planet guide that almost everything peddled through these very similar stalls was fake – even the cigars. You got what you paid for, if you wanted a Rolex for $50 what do you expect. Most of the merchandise was mass produced in the capital Santa Domingo and shipped out to the resort towns.

They parked the jeep and joined the throng of tourists jostling through the streets. For about an hour they moved around and until Max put a hand on Cass's shoulder.
"Hey, I'm frying here!" He was really struggling in the 40-degree heat. They ducked into a small bar and hid in a booth at the back.
"This is no good" Cass smiled "But I have an idea". She told Max to stay where he was. And went to the next table and said

hello to two backpackers. They were a young couple and after a few questions Cass found out they were French.

Max wondered what she was doing but didn't have to wait long to find out.

"Max this is Francois and Yvette" Cass introduced them.

"They are going to do us a little favour" Cass smiled.

Martinez's men had split into pairs and it was the two by the beach that saw Max and Cass come out of the café. They quickly called the other two on the cell-phone.

Langusto's men were back in their jeep watching the other jeep. They had figured that Max had to come back to it eventually and sure enough, they were just coming round the corner.

"Marco. Do you see those four men getting into that blue car?"

"Yeah" he said uninterested.

"One if them I recognise. It's Manny Rodriguez"

"Shit" exclaimed Marco and looked closely.

"Martinez's hitman. You'd better get on the phone and get some help"

Marco slammed the jeep into gear and sped after the blue car.

"We don't have anyone over here" Marco said solemnly.

"You're right. Let's just follow. Probably nothing will happen"

The blue car was closing in on the jeep, which was gaining speed. The road was running close to the ocean and as they emerged from the trees the jeep swerved off the road onto the beach.

"Damn" the driver of the blue car hit the brakes and the car slid in the sand. Ten seconds later the other jeep with Marco sped past the car and along the beach. Ahead of them Max's jeep had appeared to have stopped. As they got closer they could see the jeep had been abandoned and the occupants were a couple of hundred yards into the sea – even from that distance Marco knew it wasn't Kovács.

66

Max and Cass stepped off the small boat and onto the beach on Bacardi Island.

"I hope those two youngsters are ok" Cass said feeling a little guilty at putting them in danger.

"I just wish you'd have picked someone a little bigger" Max replied. Cass stopped for a moment and couldn't help laughing. The only thing that had fitted was the bamboo strip hat. The shirt left part of Max's stomach exposed – white and pasty – and the shorts were tight and he hadn't been able to get all the buttons done up.

"Oh hah hah" he said and walked awkwardly to the bar on the edge of the beach.

"As soon as the guide has finished his introduction and they all head off to the scuba diving we can get round to the other side of the island" Cass replied.

67

Allesandro Langusto smiled to himself.

'Sixty million dollars in sales, and I haven't had to kill anybody yet'

He was putting the final touches to the small arms shipments. He had needed to borrow from one of his consignments to Namibia and although that had cost him over the odds the last of the guns would be with his agent that afternoon. The phone rang and he grabbed it.

"Yes?"

It was Marco.

"What do you mean Rodriguez was in Cabarete?"

Marco was at a phone back at Puerto Plata airport.

"Just like I said, Rodriguez and three goons" Marco repeated.

"Stay put" Allesandro said and slammed the phone down. His mind was racing. Martinez was trying to screw up his deal.

'This time he had gone too far' he thought.

68

The Martinez villa was smaller than Max had expected, but he reflected that every brick would have been carried from the beach and taking that into consideration it was pretty impressive. It looked deserted but Cass wasn't taking any chances. They spent an hour and a half slowly edging around the perimeter which revealed three guards, four rooms and a wine cellar.

69

"I want a meeting" Luco said coolly. He glanced over at the
rest of the family who had all gathered in the restaurant.
Martinez was on the speakerphone so they could all hear.

"Want is a strong word". Martinez's voice was cocky and
confident.

"Five o'clock at the central library"

"Just me and you Luco?"

"Just you and me". Luco clicked off the phone and under his
breath.

"He could do with spending some time in there the little
illiterate sonofabitch".

Nobody laughed. It was well known that Luco despised
Martinez all the more because he has built his empire through
mindless violence and lack of finesse. Luco liked to think of
himself as a gentleman criminal and cited Martinez's lack of a
formal education as the reason why his methods were so
primitive.

70

Max felt useless as he sat two hundred yards from the villa.
Cass had reminded him that it was what she did, but he
couldn't help feeling worried for her. The first guard was
sitting on a tree stump reading a book when he got a blow to
the head and toppled into the undergrowth. Cass slipped around
the side of the veranda where the other two were playing cards.
She tossed a small stone in through an open window and it
clattered across the wooden floor. The two men dropped their
cards and went to draw their pistols. That was all the time Cass
needed. Neither of them saw what hit them. The first got Cass's
fist into his temple and the other her foot in his face. The first
went down like a sack of potatoes but the second stumbled
clutching his shattered nose. Cass spun around and unleashed
another kick to his midriff. This sent him back into a glass
cabinet that smashed and fell forwards on top of him.

Max could hear the commotion and headed towards the villa. Cass came out onto the front steps and motioned for him to hurry up.

71

Allesandro and Luco rode in the back of a red Cadillac to the central library. The caddy had been 'modified' with armour plating and four inch glass windows.

"I don't like this" Allesandro said.

"Even he is not so stupid to try something here"

The central library was directly opposite the main police headquarters and the square outside was packed with police cars.

The library itself was a wonderful cream building rebuilt in the 1950s. Luco pushed through the glass doors and smiled at the librarian behind the counter removing his sunglasses and hat. He could see Martinez sitting at a large oak table in the middle of the fiction section. He had his arms folded and resting on a large hardback copy of 'Das Boat'. Martinez was a wiry figure who worked out incessantly and Luco noticed that he never seemed to age much. He knew he was thirty-eight but he had to admit that he looked good for his age. His hair was shaven short and his dark eyes never left Luco's as he came over to the table and sat down.

"It has been a long time"

"Eight years" Martinez agreed. Martinez had worked for Allesandro originally running operations in Old Havana. That was until he saw more money in going independent. Martinez's band of cousins along with his two brothers gradually took ground from the Langustos. He was purely a domestic operator, but dealt plenty of drugs from most of the South American countries. He had fewer connections than Luco but made up for it in ruthlessness. Even a cold killer like Allesandro was wary of the man.

Lets cut to the chase" Luco said.

"I want you to back off my client. I have a lot riding on this - enough to risk a confrontation with you"

"Your client? And that would be?"

"You know damn well who" Luco snapped quietly.

"Indulge me" Martinez smiled.

"Okay. No bullshit. If you go anywhere near Kovács again I'm coming after you"

"Kovács? János Kovács?" Martinez let out a low long whistle. Although he only dallied at arms Martinez had heard of Kovács. Everyone had heard of Kovács.

"Come on Luco, I'm not that mad"

"Don't bullshit me. Rodriguez was on his ass yesterday"

"Rodriguez wasn't even in Havana yesterday" Martinez argued. I know he was chasing down Kovács in the Dominican."

Martinez paused for a moment then grinned.

"I heard he had a weakness for the ladies but this is priceless"

"What?" said Luco.

"Rodriguez wasn't there for Kovács. He didn't even know who the guy was. He was there to ice that little Israeli bitch"

"Katherine Derrick?" Luco asked but he was beginning to get the picture.

"She's Mossad. Israeli intelligence. She's killed one of my best men already" Martinez scowled.

'Oh shit' thought Luco. 'How could János have been so stupid. Still, she fooled all of us'

He had to find Kovács and fast. Luco got up to leave and Martinez grabbed his arm.

"If you get to her first, promise me that she will suffer. It was my cousin that she killed" Luco removed his hand from his arm.

"Don't worry. She will take a *very* long time to die" he said and headed to the door.

72

It took all of five minutes to search the four rooms and they found nothing. They had to search two of the guards before they found the keys to the pantry and the wine cellar.

"Max" Cass shouted to him as he checked the pantry.

"There are boat keys on this set. You check the cellar and I'll find the boat"

"Oh and take these"

She tossed one of the guards' pistols and a torch and ran out onto the porch. Max unlocked the thick wooden door with a big iron key and it creaked open.

There were about twenty steps down and Max shone the torch into the darkness. He guessed the villa had been built on top of a rock and that they had used a natural cave as the basis for the cellar. It was slightly damp and Max took care not to slip on the steps as he made his way down slowly. He reached the bottom and found himself in a main room with three rooms off it. Each had a wooden door similar to the one at the top of the stairs except these had been cut to fit the openings in the rock.

One of the doors was open and when he shone his light in Max could see that from the floor to the ceiling were racks full of dusty wine bottles. Max opened the second door and found a large storage room and moved on to the third. That one was locked and it took Max a few guesses with the bunch of keys before he found the right one. The room was small and very dark. Max shone the torch around. In the corner was a mattress with a pile of rocks on it. Max stepped closer and the pile of rocks moved. The bunched up figure on the mattress was shielding its eyes from the light.

"Pete?" Max whispered. This thin figure couldn't be him.

"Mmmmm" the figure mumbled and Max gently lifted him into a sitting position. Max could hardly recognise Pete's face. He'd been so badly beaten it was little wonder that he could only mumble. His left eye was completely closed from swelling and his left arm hung limply by his side.

"Pete. It's Max mate. You're ok now"

Max checked him over briefly and he guessed a broken collarbone, at least two cracked ribs but at least his legs seemed in tact. He got Pete to his feet and helped him through the door.

It took a few minutes to get to the top of the steps and Max heard Cass call.

"Max, we'd better get out of here. You find anything?"

Max walked onto the veranda and Pete's legs gave way.

"Jesus" Cass exclaimed as she saw Pete.

"We'd better get him to a hospital" Max said. Cass nodded.

"Their boat will get us back to Puerto Plata. I've tied the three of them together but no doubt someone will realise soon".

Max put Pete over his shoulder and carefully they headed to the boat.

"There was enough in the house to take down Martinez" Cass said as they got to the speedboat.

'Well at least we have that' Max thought and smiled. They laid Pete flat on the floor of the boat and sped away from the island.

73

"Any news" Allesandro asked as Luco walked back in to the lounge.

"Nothing" he replied.

It had been eight hours now and it was beginning to get dark. In less than two days they were due to complete an extremely profitable deal which wasn't going to happen unless they found their client.

74

When they got to Puerto Plata, Max phoned the British Embassy in Santa Domingo and explained that Pete had been in a car accident and his documents were missing. He arranged for a private hospital in Mexico city. It was close enough until they could get him back to New York. They couldn't risk using the main airport themselves so Pete boarded the plane on a stretcher accompanied by two nurses.

75

"Where to Senor?" asked the cab driver.

"Santa Domingo" Max replied.

"No" said Cass.

"Himenetta" she told the cab driver. Max turned to Cass.

"Why Himenetta?" he asked. He'd never heard of the place but it sounded small.

"We can charter a plane to get us back to Havana" she replied.

"You must be kidding. It's over. We've found Pete, you've got Martinez. Time to go home" Even as he finished the sentence Max could see the look in her eyes.

"Without you I can't get back into the Langustos"

"Suits me, you'll be safe" Max said.

"Its what I do Max. I can't, and I won't change that"

Max sighed.

"One more evening at The Langustos. The deal doesn't hit until Monday so we could be out of the country tomorrow," she added.

He wasn't convinced but nodded slowly.

76

Allesandro and Luco were sitting on the veranda when Luco's cell-phone chirped.

"Visitors at the gate sir".

Luco checked his watch, seven p.m.

"Who is it?" he snapped.

"Senor Kovács and the Senora. Shall I let them in"

Luco put his hand over the receiver.

"It's him" he said in a surprised voice "and the Israeli is with him"

"She's with him?"

"I forgot they were coming to dinner".

Luco waved them quiet.

"Si, si bring them in," he said quickly.

Marco stood up with his pistol drawn.

"Hey" Allesandro said. "She doesn't know we know about her. Lets play it clever"

Max and Cass came into view across the lounge.

"János, how was your day?" Luco asked as they stepped onto the veranda.

"Did a little touristing on the islands" Max smiled.

"Their cigars are definitely not as good as yours" he laughed.

Luco joined in. "Drink?" he asked and motioned to Marco.

"Yeah. Could do with a scotch. I must be getting paranoid but I could have sworn we were followed today".

Allesandro glanced at Luco.

"Bloody inconvenience. Lost one jeep and had to hire another one" he laughed.

"Its better safe than sorry" Luco said as he handed Max his scotch.

77

Dinner was a quieter affair than the previous evenings – pizzas on the veranda. Max wondered how many of the Langustos were out searching for him.

'They must have been going nuts' he thought.

They had dessert out by the bar that was lit with dozens of small lamps as the light was fading. As Max had tried to sit down Cass had shuffled him into a chair facing the bar with his back against one of the four pillars of the barbecue area. After a few drinks Cass disappeared off to the powder room.

78

Baber was sitting at his new desk in Skopje feeling sorry for himself. His laptop beeped and he saw he had a PDA message. He clicked open the box and a single line of text stared back at him.

M: Planes @ Gresnock airfield, S.Africa.

79

"Get your hands off me" Cass screamed as Marco dragged her through the house by her hair. He threw her against the bar and Max turned as she clattered onto the floor.

"What's the meaning of this!" he shouted.

"Perhaps Mrs.Derrick would like to explain" Marco snapped back.

"János" Luco said and placed a hand on his shoulder.

"She's a spy," he said coldly.

Max froze. They knew. 'Shit!' he thought.

"A spy?" he asked trying to buy some time.

"Si. A very good one it seems"

"How could I have been so stupid" Max shouted and flung his scotch glass so it smashed a foot away from Cass's head. He grabbed her by the shoulders. Marco lunged forward but Allesandro motioned him to wait.

"What did you find out bitch!" he screamed as he shook her. Cass spat in his face.

"Nothing you pig!" she shouted, then whispered.

"Hit me and throw me over the bar quickly". Max was stunned but did as he was told. He hit her hard across the face and she let out a wince of pain. Marco smiled. He was glad Allesandro had called him off. Max grabbed Cass's shoulders again and threw her over the bar. She crashed into a couple of bottles and disappeared behind the bar.

"Come here you bitch!" he shouted and went behind the bar.

"What now?" he whispered. Cass shook the glass out of her hair and checked her watch. 'Another twenty seconds' Max was confused but stood up and began kicking the underside of the bar.

"Come on you whore, get up!" he shouted. The Langusto brothers looked on and Luco thought.

"He's a vicious bastard all right" he turned to make a comment to Allesandro but he didn't get a chance.

The explosion ripped the side of the house apart and four of the Langustos were thrown into the bar with huge force. Max was pinned against the back of the bar and was hit on the shoulder by an ashtray. His head smacked into the bar wall. Rubble rained down on the veranda and a large section of the railing overhanging the canyon had been blown away.

Cass leapt up and checked the surroundings. The blast had caved in the main roof and taken out the four walls of the library. There were books everywhere. There was screaming from inside the house and Maria came running out with Luco's wife Anna. They rushed to their respective husbands who were both at least unconscious.

'Worse I hope' thought Cass. She quickly took a piece of glass and sliced her forehead and smeared the blood across her face.

"Get an ambulance" she screamed at the two women and Maria ran back into the house. Max was trying to get up and Cass gave him a hand.

"What the fuck was that!" he stammered.

"Come on" she shouted at him and dragged him into the house.

"Where are we going?" he managed to get out as they raced up the stairs. Before he got an answer Cass kicked open a door and Max saw they were on the roof. In front of them were two power gliders.

"Surely not?" he said as Cass pushed him towards the closer one.

"You told me you'd flown one of these before" she complained.

"That was ten years ago, and besides I was with an instructor on a fun flight, not two thousand feet up a bloody mountain".

"Can you start it?" she asked as she strapped herself on behind him.

"I think so" Max replied and pressed the ignition. The hang glider roared into life but they didn't move.

"Well?" she shouted.

"Brakes I think" Max shouted back and he tried all the levers until the glider lunged forward and off the roof. Within a second they were flying alongside the canyon with the villa a smouldering heap behind them.

They heard the engine of the second glider kick-in and Cass turned around to see the glider leave the roof.

"Step on it" she shouted to Max.

Max was trying desperately not to look down. Not that he could see much below them in the half-light.

"How are we supposed to land in the dark?" he shouted.

"Just fly it" Cass screamed and clutched the pistol she had taken from Marco's body. She suspected Marco wad dead due to the huge piece of glass embedded in his back.

She fired a couple of shots that drew a dozen or so in return. A couple were close, with one clipping the metal frame of the glider making an annoying pinging sound.

"Don't worry" Cass screamed. "They won't be here for long" she laughed. Sure enough within a few seconds they heard the engine of the other glider splutter band cut off. The two figures inside tried desperately to restart the engine but it was dead. Cass had cut the fuel line when she had discovered the hand gliders earlier.

Max let out a sigh of relief that proved premature. Whatever weapons the two had grabbed they now employed at Max and Cass.

They were too far away to aim but the odds were high that one of the dozens of shots would hit the mark.

Max felt the sharp pain in his side and for a moment let go of the controls. He gritted his teeth and grasped the controls again. He had not been shot before and although in a lot of pain, had expected it to be worse.

He shouted back to Cass

"I'm hit in the side".

He thought he heard her reply "I know" and twisted his head around to see Cass slumped back in her seat. There was lots of blood on her dress at the same height as his wound.

"It went through her before it hit me," Max said to himself. He turned back to the front and continued to follow the side of the mountain towards Havana.

80

The scene at the Langusto house had calmed down. Luco was still unconscious; Allessandro was talking to one of the two men in the glider on his cell-phone. They had landed on the main road up to the villa and were waiting for Allesandro to reach them in a car.

The ambulance was on its way, though it would be a good twenty miles at best. Marco was alone, just. The huge piece of glass was still embedded in his back. Allessandro knowing not to remove it in case it had severed an artery.

"Get every available man and when they land kill them" he shouted.

He closed his phone and went to Luco's side again. He didn't like the look of his big brother. He had been a mound of rubble and was looking like his back might be broken so they decided not to move him. He and Marco lay where they had fallen.

He swore under his breath. "You will pay for this Kovács!"

81

Max was starting to feel dizzy. He knew he was over Havana, he knew the Langustos would be searching for their glider but most of all he knew he was slowly losing blood. In a moment of inspiration he turned the glider around and headed for the castle.

The El Morro Castle was built in 1589 and is a very popular tourist attraction. At night it is lit up beautifully. This feature made it very easy to see from the air at night. The other important attribute of the castle is that it was within a quarter of a mile of the British Embassy. It wasn't as big or lavish as many of the other Embassies around the world but nevertheless it had a large Union Jack flying above it and Max hoped that once circling the castle he would be able to see it.

The Langustos' men had located the glider in the sky and had two cars tracking it through the streets. It was too public to take a shot but once they landed they would have them.

82

Martin Beaumont was extremely bored. To say that Cuba was an uneventful posting was an understatement. It was a good stepping stone he kept telling himself.

Deputy Ambassador here and maybe, if he was lucky, Ambassador of a small country somewhere next, he just needed to keep his nose clean which wasn't going to be difficult here. He looked out of the window and smiled as he looked down to the car park where his 1956 dark blue Chevy gleamed in the lights of the Embassy. Now that was one perk he did like.

He watched in horror as a large contraption skidded across the car park and slammed into the side of the Chevy. He ran down the staircase to the lobby. He hesitated at the front door peering through to check the scene.

The four guards stood about twenty feet from what looked like some sort of glider. They had their weapons drawn but were understandably reluctant to get any closer.

The fabric of the glider moved a little and a large man in a cream jacket staggered out and fell onto the ground.

"Put your hands up" shouted one of the guards and steadied his pistol with both hands. Max looked up into the man's eyes then across to the front doors straight at Beaumont.

"Get a Doctor" Max said.

"I said put your hands up sir," the guard said louder this time.

Max got to his feet, put his hands above his head and walked straight to Beaumont.

"You look like a sensible fella," Max said quickly as he stood three steps below.

"Please get a Doctor and fast".

"There is an Israeli diplomat in the glider. She's been shot and if she doesn't get medical attention she might die, and you wouldn't want that would you?"

Beaumont was taken aback.

"Peterson" he shouted over his shoulder. "Get out here".

"Thank you" Max said.

"You just keep your hands up," Beaumont said in a stern voice". He noticed the man's shirt was covered in blood.

A young man with a doctor's bag ran out to the front doors, with two of the guards he lifted Cass out of the glider.

"Martin" Peterson shouted back to the doors.

"She's lost a lot of blood. She needs a hospital".

"No" Max snapped. "Do you have a medical bay"

"Yes, but its not that well equipped. Besides who the hell are you" Beaumont said turning to Max.

"Look just get her stable and we can call London".

"What you're a spook?" Beaumont said.

"A spy? Not Exactly" Max said.

Peterson and the guards were carrying Cass past Max and he turned to Beaumont again.

"One call to MI5 and its sorted" Max said.

As he spoke a half a dozen police cars came speeding around the corner and lights blazing pulled up at the gates.

"Sir" a woman came running up to Beaumont.

"It's the Chief of Police on the phone. He says he wants his two prisoners back".

"Oh wonderful" Beaumont said clasping his hands together.

"Tell him he'll have to wait a few minutes".

"And get me Tina Althorpe on the phone."

"Peterson, get the man searched and see to his side" he added.

Max forced a smile and then passed out. The medical bay in the Embassy only had two beds and tonight both were full. Max was awake and looking over at Cass who was in a bad way. They had cleaned the wound and concluded that, although no organs had been hit by the bullet they had removed from Max's side she needed to get to the hospital.

Beaumont walked into the medical bay and gave Max an uneasy smile.

"We have a bit of a Mexican stand-off here."

"London have acknowledged that they would like to get you and the young lady across to the US safely.

"However the local authorities insist you are not going anywhere."

"What does the Doctor say about Cass" Max said slowly.

"She's extremely weak" Beaumont replied.

"We have to get her to a hospital before the morning."

"Thanks" said Max.

"Let me talk to the police."

83

Max's mind was racing. In five minutes he would be talking with Manton. He did not have time to go through the documents and disks Cass had taken from Allessandro's office. They sat on the table next to her bed. He wondered how good his bluff could be?

'It'd better be bloody good" he thought and got up

"Kovács" sneered Manton voice on the intercom. He was standing twenty feet from the Chief of Police and the huge guards in between them gave him little comfort.

"A lot of people want you dead" Manton continued.

"Tell me something new" Max growled.

"You have nowhere to go Mr Kovács. Stop wasting everyone's time and I give you my guarantee that you and the Israeli will die quickly."

"How long have you been in the police force?" Max asked.

"Twenty five years" said Manton proudly.

"And have you seen the inside of Havana's jails?"

"Oh you won't see those Mr.Kovács"

"I was thinking of you actually," Max said.

"We have documents from Allesandro's office with your name all over them"

"Bullshit!" Manton snapped.

"Just give him a ring" Max replied and hung up.

Max waited by the intercom. It was the longest five minutes of his life.

Manton had a problem. He weighed up the facts. He knew about the explosion at the villa. He knew Kovács had gained access to Allesandro's office. He also knew that Allessandro kept detailed accounts. He had been involved in a lot of heavy shit in the past. If he went to Allessandro he would deny it either way, but if the Hungarian was going to take the Langustos down anyway he would do well to distance himself from them.

"Okay" Manton said as Max held the intercom to his ear once more.

"I want a statement signed by you and the Ambassador giving me immunity from all aspects of this should anything get out". Max let out a long deep breath.

"You got it. In return I want a police helicopter and a jet waiting at the airport with fuel, a medical crew and facilities on board".

"Okay. You are a ruthless calculating bastard Kovács" Manton said with a hint of respect in his voice.

Max glanced back toward the embassy where Cass lay pale and fighting for her life.

"Its what I do" he said simply and hung up the phone.

84

Max stayed by Cass's side through the night on the plane and once she had been set up in a hospital bed in Mexico City. She had received a blood transfusion and was still on an IV but the hospital staff was pleased with her progress. The following morning at about six am Max was sitting in an armchair at the side of her bed. He still held her hand despite having drifted off about an hour before. He opened his eyes and stretched his back. His side was still sore and he winced a little. He glanced at Cass who had her eyes open and was smiling at him.

"Hey" he said quietly.

"Hey" she whispered back.

"How long have you been awake" he said and held her hand in both of his.

"A while" she said, "I didn't want to wake you"

"Listen to her. Watching over me again" he smiled.

"Where are the papers?" she asked.

"Oh they're here. Yesterday I made copies of everything and put them in a safety deposit box. I sent a second copy over to Easton. He wants to talk to us".

"I bet he does" Cass's eyes lit up.

"Did you find out what the Yukon base was?" she added.

"Yep. When I saw it on lots of the paperwork I checked with Martin at the NY Times. Apparently he's been sitting on an amazing story from a small-town lawyer, Petra something. Her research shows a huge link between a Chicago based company and the base. It's a US air base and most of the Langustos arms seemed to pass through there".

"I knew it!" she exclaimed.

"The irony. The US government involved with Cuban arms dealers" she shook her head in amazement.

"Oh that's not the half of it" Max leaned over and grabbed a couple of sheets of paper from a folder on the windowsill.

"Look who else is involved"

Cass took the papers and scanned over them. Her eyes reached the box on the bottom right hand corner. She lowered the sheets and looked straight into Max's eyes.

"Oh my God" she said slowly.

85

The Director of the CIA was enjoying a rare escape from his office and the fact that he had lofted an 8 iron shot from the seventh tee to the edge of the green meant that he was enjoying it all the more. He passed the club to his caddy, got into the golf cart and the driver set off down the fairway. Thirty yards ahead of them a dark suited man raised his hand to his ear and reached inside his jacket. As the cart got nearer he raised his hand and the driver slowed. The suit handed a small silver cellphone to the Director.

"Yes?" he snapped. "What do you mean I'd better take the call. Can't you deal with it?" he was annoyed at having his 'quality time' disturbed.

"Ok, put him through"

The voice on the other end of the line spoke clearly and with conviction.

"Very interesting Mr.Jones" the Director said when the caller finally finished.

"And in return for your discretion, you would be wanting how much?"

The Director of the CIA steadied himself and removed his sunglasses. He knew Jones was genuine. He'd had the briefing. He had not been expecting to take the call himself as he had assumed it would be about money, and a lot of it. It wasn't. "Your demands have a note of finality," he said.
"Yes" replied Max. "That they do. Let's just call it my contribution to prosperity" he added and hung up.

86

Pete wasn't sleeping. He was just resting his eyes. His strength had gradually come back to him but his ribs were sore and heavily strapped. He opened his eyes at the knock on the door.

"Come in" he shouted.

The door flung open and Max stormed in pushing Cass in a wheelchair.

"Max!" Pete exclaimed and grimaced in pain.

"Hey buddy, take it easy" Max laughed and came round to the side of the bed.

"No time for that. We have a present for you"

"We?" Pete smiled across at Cass.

"Oh, sorry this is Cass. Cass, this is Pete"

"Hi Pete" Cass said giving him a wink.

"You look much better" she smiled.

"Come on, come on" Max said "Open it".

He thrust a large box into Pete's hands.

"Quick" Max said.

Pete pulled off the ribbon and lifted the lid of the box. Inside was a laptop connected to a mobile phone. The screen was on and the familiar blue and yellow figure of the Roving Reporter was at the top.

"Roving Reporter" Pete smiled.

"Go on then. Click on it" Max urged.

Pete moved the mouse and clicked on the icon and a video and text box opened in the middle of the screen. The video box had a pair of white doors in the centre of the picture. Max handed Pete a sheet of paper and a keyboard connected to a PDA.

"Go on then. Get typing" Max said to Pete who shrugged and started.

87

The two men studied each other across the large table. They had dismissed the guards from the room about five minutes before and had sat in silence. The younger man gestured towards the ornate coffee set at the end of the room. The old man nodded and George got out of his seat and poured two cups of steaming black coffee. He put one in front of the old man and took a seat at his side. He cradled the coffee cup in his hands and stared deep into the thick black liquid as if looking for inspiration.

"I suppose you are as uncomfortable with this as I am?" he said.

The old man took a sip from his cup and sighed.

"I have seen sparks of revolution and years of defiance, but somehow in my heart I knew this day would come".

George nodded and lifted the cup to his lips and paused.

"Did you think it would come in your lifetime?" he asked.

The old man shook his head slowly.

"No" he said solemnly. "We are sure this is unavoidable?" he added but he already knew the answer. George nodded and they both rose and headed towards the big white doors. George put his hand on the old man's shoulder as he reached for the door. "Come on. Let's make history".

88

You are here live with Pete Smalt on this historic occasion. You join us at The Whitehouse where in a few moments time history will be changed forever. Two nations who have been separated by a huge political divide have broken down the barriers.

Pete looked at Max who motioned for him to keep going.

In an exclusive interview with the two leaders they gave the reasons for the shock announcements. Relations have been improving slowly over the past decade and with a major recession looming the trade opportunity for both could not be ignored.

The white doors in the video stream opened and George W. Bush and Fidel Castro stepped out onto The Whitehouse lawn. They smiled and shook hands in front of the single video camera - and the 127 million people watching on their PCs across the world.

The End

Cuban Cut

&

Cut To The Chase

are both available as e-books in Palm™ and PDF formats with
the help of DigitalWrite – links to e-bookshops from
www.cubancut.com

Details of opportunities for other UK writers
are available at www.mxpublishing.com

This book was written by Steve Emecz and is representative of
a completely digital workflow. It was created, proofed, printed
and finally stored digitally for future on demand reprints.

The covers were printed on the DocuColor 2060 using
Xerox Colortech paper. The text was imposed using Preps
software and then printed using Xerox Publisher paper on the
DocuTech Book Factory. The covers were introduced and the
3 knife trim completed the story, if you see what I mean.

Please enjoy this complimentary copy.